GHOSTS
COME
RISING

ADAM PERRY

**YELLOW
JACKET**

YELLOW JACKET
an imprint of Little Bee Books

New York, NY
Copyright @ 2022 by Adam Perry
All rights reserved, including the right of
reproduction in whole or in part in any form.
Yellow Jacket and associated colophon are
trademarks of Little Bee Books.
Interior designed by Natalie Padberg Bartoo
For information about special discounts on bulk purchases,
please contact Little Bee Books at sales@littlebeebooks.com.
Manufactured in China RRD 0522
First Edition
10 9 8 7 6 5 4 3 2 1
Library of Congress Cataloging-in-Publication
Data is available upon request.
ISBN 978-1-4998-1354-8
yellowjacketreads.com

Photo illustrations were created using a mix of original photography, assets from BigStockPhoto.com, and historical images from the Library of Congress, whose original photographers are listed below. (C) Harris & Ewing, Miss Libby, National Photo Company; (pg. iv) Arnold Genthe, C.M. Bell; (pg. 5) Arnold Genthe, Harris & Ewing; (pg. 61) Arnold Genthe , Harris & Ewing; (pg. 93) Historic American Buildings Survey, Mountain Home Air Force Base; (pg. 153) Antony Barboza collection, C.M. Bell, Marion Post Wolcott; (pg. 183) C.M. Bell; (pg. 276) C.M. Bell, John Vachon, National Photo Company

To my grandparents

In the mid-nineteenth century, a religious movement called Spiritualism spread across America. Spiritualists believe that the living can communicate with the dead.

Though it faded in popularity in the beginning of the twentieth century, it returned at the end of the First World War and the emergence of the Spanish Flu Pandemic, when many people were looking to make a connection with their loved ones, no matter the cost.

Though many mediums in the movement were later revealed to be frauds, it is unknown if any were telling the truth.

PROLOGUE

With a twist of my fingers, I can raise the dead.

Watch me work in the darkness, going through a stack of newsprint photographs, cutting out faces and arranging them on the table. My fingers move quickly, acting from the memories baked deep in my muscles. I glue a face and a swirl of cotton to a black-painted board, and just like that, a ghost is formed.

Enough to fool people, anyway.

I hold my creation up to be judged. Sometimes my younger brother, John, stands behind me and clucks in approval; other times he adds little comments like, *Her head don't look right*, or, *You cut that one sloppy*.

He's always right.

I move on, and when I look over my shoulder, I see John's sunken eyes in the candlelight, and I think he looks more like a ghost than any of the ones I create.

He coughs until he shakes, and I rub his back to settle him.

"Breathe, John."

"I'm all right. Keep working."

My camera is as thin as a book when closed, and I unhook the side and extend the bellows like an accordian. I light the lantern's wick and move it close, so the face is exposed, then turn the lens until the blur is right.

Things look magical out of focus.

Click. The shutter opens long enough to soak in a hint of light and the first exposure is made on a plate of photographic glass, just enough for the imagination to work.

Out in the hall, I hear Mr. Spencer's speech, polished from hundreds of performances:

"Come, oh spirit! Descend upon this room! Join us for a moment on this side."

I mouth along, can tell when he's been drinking by the rhythm of the words.

When the time is right, I open the small door and deliver a package to Mr. Spencer. My dark hair and clothes blend into the background. I'm never even seen.

By the time he slides it into his camera the con is finished and—

Click.

The second exposure is made in the studio, this one lit by a flash.

"The camera will never leave your sight," Mr.

Spencer says to the woman. "There are some who doubt the truth of what I do, but we know better. Make no mistake, your husband is here with us right now. Surely you feel his spirit reaching out to you. Follow me, we'll develop it together."

He charges ten dollars a photo, by appointment only. It seems expensive, but Mr. Spencer tells me they're rich folk, except they don't look it to me.

"Never leave my side. I want you to know this is real," Mr. Spencer says.

Real. Mr. Spencer says the word over and over, as if repeating it will make it so. And maybe if you tell yourself a story enough times, you really *can* believe it. Maybe the lies we tell ourselves are the strongest kind, the kind that makes you ignore all the signs pointing at the truth.

Time passes, and from the darkroom I hear a shriek of joy as the woman sees an image appear on glass, watching as a ghost comes rising from the dead, almost like her husband was never really gone.

I smile. My work was good.

The days turn into weeks in this town—the eighteenth place we've been since we started living with Mr. Spencer—and John and I go through more papers and take more photos, always dressed in dark clothes and hidden away in closets or back rooms. We're ghost children that hide in the shadows.

Cut, cut, cut.

Glue, glue, glue.

Click, click, click.

When it's dark, we lie on a narrow mattress in the back room. I always sleep, dreamless, with John's body wrapped in my arms, like we did when we were back home. *One soul in two bodies*, our parents used to say, before the sickness took them.

I hold him tighter. John breathes heavy, but I think he's getting better. Maybe that's another story that I want to believe.

Some nights I think about what we're doing and wonder if it's bad. But I do it for him, and that's all that matters. I'll say anything if it keeps him with me.

My name is Liza Carroll. I'm twelve years old.

My brother, John, is ten.

Don't believe anything I say.

PART ONE

A THIN PLACE

RUNAWAY

Our cab bounces over a dirt road. The grass along it is long and wet with morning dew. It's cold, and through the windows I can see the horses snorting white steam. The inside of the cab smells like wax and the stale vapors of Mr. Spencer's drink. He's sleeping again, even though it's morning and the sun is beating through the window and the grassy hills are a radiant yellow. He sleeps a lot, and his hands shake. More than a tremble, more than last year.

John coughs and leans into my arm.

"Where we goin' now?" he asks.

"Don't know."

"Don't he tell you nothing?"

"Doesn't," I correct him. I lean into his face and whisper, "And you know he doesn't tell me anything."

John smiles. He's small for his age, and his eyes remind me of our mother's.

"Well, where were we before?"

"New York," I answer, though we were far away

from the city with tall buildings I'd seen in books.

He sits up and peers out the window.

"Sun's that way, so we're heading south. You reckon we're in Florida by now?"

"That's too far. We're probably still in New York. It's a big state."

"Quiet, Liza," Mr. Spencer says, kicking his foot against our seat. He licks his lips and crosses his hands over his chest. "We're going to Pennsylvania."

I don't know how long he's been listening to us.

Pennsylvania, John mouths, smiling at me.

I think back to what Mr. Spencer told me last night.

"Where we're going is the jewel of the east," he had said. I could see his shadow blocking out the sliver of moonlight under the door. "A hidden gold mine. Riches beyond our grandest dreams if we can prove ourselves. Their endorsement will mean steady work wherever we go. Don't ruin it, Liza."

John stares into my eyes, seeming to read my thoughts. His head bounces up and down with the movement of the cab.

"What else did he tell you?" he asks.

It's hard to remember. He said other things to me, but I didn't listen to him, just repeated, *Don't ruin it, Liza*, until the words lost their meaning.

"Nothing," I whisper.

We've been with Mr. Spencer for nearly three years now, and the man is still a mystery to me. He's our closest living relative according to the courts, first cousin to our father. He's a liar and a fraud, but I think the biggest con he ever pulled was convincing the judge he was a respectable adult, able to take care of children. He presents himself well in small bits, and I admit I was taken in, too, by this thin man in the black suit, long gray beard and hair combed right down the middle with thick grease.

"I will teach you *business,*" he said that first day as soon as we were out of the courthouse and back out on the street, drawing out the word like a hissing snake.

Mr. Spencer was a photographer then, much as he is now, and a rotten one at that, though it paid for his way of life. Those were the days you could call yourself a photographer just by owning a camera, and he happened to have two identical ones, which I always guessed he stole from a shop or won in a card game.

He didn't have an eye for proper photography—his landscapes were poorly framed, and his portraits were blurry and dark, which is probably why it's come to this, cheating people out of their money for our photographs.

Now, we ride on to our next stop, where a fresh batch of people are waiting.

We've been traveling all through the night, first in a small carriage out of the city and then on a train that took us in tunnels carved through mountains and out into rolling farmlands. When the train stopped, a horse-drawn cab was waiting for us at the station, and it's almost like we've stepped back in time, far away from the cities and towns we've traveled to before.

We didn't stay long in that last place. Things always go bad eventually, no matter where we go. Someone calls Mr. Spencer a fraud and then others join in, daring him to take a picture with equipment they provide, before I can do my work. Mr. Spencer refuses, of course. He makes up some excuse, and we pack our bags before they chase us out of town with sticks and guns and unchristian words. I'm good at sensing when something's about to go wrong, can feel it in my stomach like a pot of boiling water, and things were starting to bubble. I think of the man in the alleyway who approached me and John. *Are you with Mr. Spencer? I just have some questions*, he said.

That's always how it starts. Some questions.

Through the window of the cab, the trees sink behind us. It doesn't look like anyone's following us, and Mr. Spencer seems to know what I'm thinking.

"That detective is far behind us," he says. His eyes are open now and staring through me. "We don't have to worry about him anymore. Did he see you?"

"No," I lie. *What's his secret?* the man yelled before John and I ran and hid.

"Are you sure?"

"I promise."

I itch in my black dress, and John closes his eyes as the cab rattles on. We travel for hours, moving over giant hills and through lanes surrounded by trees until we get to uneven roads that lead to fields peppered with small farms and barns.

When the sun is higher in the sky, it hits the window just right and the inside of the cab starts to heat up. I wish I didn't need to wear this awful dress, but this time is different. This time he can't let on that he knows me. *Stop number nineteen.*

Mr. Spencer knocks on the side of the cab and tells the driver to stop.

"You remember the plan?" he asks me.

"Same story as in Lansing?"

Mr. Spencer nods. "You're a runaway. But don't talk so much this time. You can never keep your stories straight."

I nod, thinking back to the directions he whispered

to me through the door, before we ran in the dead of night.

He opens the cab door, and I hop outside and open the trunk. My brown suitcase is wedged between Mr. Spencer's case and the side of the cab. It's a big old thing, and it takes me three strong tugs to get it out.

The horses kick in place, impatient.

"Bye, Liza," John says. He has tears in his eyes, and I feel bad leaving him alone with Mr. Spencer.

"Don't cry, silly, I'll be there real soon. You won't forget me, will you?"

He smiles and mouths, *I love you.*

I love you, too, I mouth back.

"Go that way," Mr. Spencer whispers, mindful of the driver's attention. He waves his hand like a hatchet toward the woods of red and orange trees. "We're four miles out, maybe five. You'll know it when you see it. Biggest house around. Wait until the sun is going down. I should be settled in by then."

He knocks again. The driver whips the reins, and the horses start to pull. I blow a kiss to John, and the driver looks at me with a raised eyebrow, but he knows better than to ask questions. He's been paid not to. The cab moves on, down the road until it's little more than a dot.

I'm alone now, and I let the silence sink in, listen to the birds and rustling leaves.

Slinking into the woods, I catch my dress on a thorny vine, and it leaves a long rip down the side. I circle back, run through the thorns again, watch as the small spikes tear the silk fabric and cut the skin across my knee. Blood runs down my leg.

Would the girl that owned this dress before me ever notice it was gone? Probably not. She had dozens in the dresser, and she never saw me sneak into her room. Anyway, she's far away now. I take one more trip through the thorns until I'm thoroughly scraped, and then I keep walking, watching the sun, heading in the direction Mr. Spencer pointed.

It's been so long since I've eaten, and my whole body tingles. Some berries grow from a bush, but I know better than to eat them. I grab a few and squish them between my fingers, smear the red on my cheeks and wipe the remainder through my hair.

Deeper in the woods, there's a stream surrounded by poison ivy. Mother told me how to spot it by counting the leaves, and I carefully step around it and through the water, but my legs start itching all the same.

"It's all in your mind," I say out loud. It feels good to hear something out in this silence.

I have time to waste, so I sit on the bank and run

my toes in the cold water and watch for animals deep in the woods. I see a rabbit hopping over twigs, and the dark tail of some bigger creature running away from me. I have a brief thought of being eaten alive, torn apart by a pack of ravenous wolves. Mr. Spencer wouldn't ever think of me again, I'd bet. John's the only one in the world who would care, and what would Mr. Spencer do with him if I wasn't there? I'm the only one keeping him alive.

More rustling comes from the trees, so I press on. The woods look the same in every direction. I can't see the road anymore. Which way did I come? Mr. Spencer said it was four miles out, but I don't know how far I've gone, and how would he know, anyway? I've never heard him mention Pennsylvania in his stories, so I suspect he's never been here. I force myself to breathe.

Don't ruin it, Liza. Don't ruin it.

The stream must lead somewhere, so I walk beside it, and by the time I break out of the woods, I'm good and dirty and I have a bunch of small rips on my dress. The blood on my knee has dried a dark red all the way down to my ankle.

There's a hill of long grass to the right and I scale it, digging my feet into the earth. My suitcase is heavy, and I pass the handle back and forth between my hands when one side starts to hurt. The sun is high in the sky and I'm tired, but there's still a long wait until it's dark and I can make my appearance.

Following the dirt road, I see a small lane branching off through pokeweed, leading to a barn surrounded by long wooden fences. Cows graze around and chew and sleep.

There's no one around. Maybe that's a good place for a runaway to hide.

THE HIDDEN PLACE

Inside, the barn is dark and musty and smells so bad that I cough and cover my face with my hand. A barrel full of tools sits by the door, and there's a dirty shovel propped into a pile of straw. The stalls are all empty, and there's a loft on the far side.

I sit down in a corner and rest my suitcase between my legs. It's the only nice thing I have, all brown and leather, with brass along the edges. I flip the latches open and push aside my small selection of clothes to reveal a tan bottom, though if you measured the depth on the inside and the size of the outside, you'd know the numbers don't add up. I rub my fingers along the side, feel for the seams, and pry it up to reveal the secret compartment, a few inches deep.

I scan the contents, making sure everything's there. The camera, my knives, cotton and glue, the black-painted board, a book of matches, a spool of string, a stack of yellowed photographs, along with other odds and ends I've stolen along the way.

I take everything out, refold, rearrange, count the pieces as if some of it might disappear if I don't check it again and again. Maybe I should try to sleep. I didn't get much of it last night, not on the noisy train or in the rattling cab. The barn floor is hard, but I arrange a pile of straw and circle it like a dog, trying to find a way to get—

"Freeze," a voice says.

Out of the loft, a boy's head rises. His eyes are wide like two little moons, and his yellow hair is as stiff and unkempt as the straw pile. He points a BB gun at me.

"What're you doin' here?" he asks, trying to make his voice sound deeper than it is.

I slide my suitcase behind me and stand.

"Good day," I say, as pleasant as I can muster.

"Who are you?" He cocks the gun.

"Is that a Daisy rifle?" I ask, unfazed by his threat. His aim is off, and he can't hold his hands steady.

"Markham," he says, looking down at the name on the stock, and I start climbing the ladder.

"Stop it!"

"Oh, you're not going to shoot me, and we both know it."

I pull myself onto the loft and he backs up, holding the gun across his chest like a shield. Now that I'm closer I realize he's as old as me, though he's shorter and skinnier. He has a thin face and kind eyes, though he tries hide that.

"Do you live here, or are you running away too?" I ask.

He blinks, stunned at the question.

"Running away? You're a runaway?" he asks, lowering his voice.

"Didn't I just say that?"

I sit down, stretch out my legs like I own the place and he's the one that's visiting.

"Where you runnin' from?" he asks.

"Florida," I say, mainly because that's the first state on my mind.

"Ain't that far away?"

"It is, but I hopped a train and rode it north. Been wandering around for days, looking for a spot to stay. Where's this?"

"Pennsylvania," he says, sitting across from me, a snake enchanted by the charmer's flute. "Right outside of Glensboro. You came all this way on your own?"

"So what if I did?" I say, stepping closer, waving my hand at the gun. "Let me see that."

He doesn't oblige.

"What was in that case of yours?" he asks, and suddenly I feel exposed, like all my secrets are there to be pulled apart and displayed for his greedy eyes.

"Nothing. Just some clothes and other things. Whatever I managed to take from home 'fore I ran away."

"Looked like you had a knife," he says.

I cluck my tongue.

"That's my Hidden Place. Isn't a girl allowed to have some secrets?" I ask, and try to change the topic of conversation. "What's your name?"

"George," he says. "You?"

"Violet," I tell him. My mother's name. "What are you doing out here with a gun?"

"Shooting," he says, and on cue, a gray bird flaps its wings against the barn ceiling and settles on the edge of a triangle-shaped window. "They leave a mess all over the floor, and Pa says I either got to deal with them with my gun or clean it up with the mop."

George props the gun on the loft rail and hunches over. He squints his eye and holds his breath, exhales and squeezes the trigger. The shot is off by a foot, and the bird flaps and flies out the window and away.

I start laughing and George's face turns red. He stares at me with his mouth hanging wide open.

"You made me miss!"

"Did not. You got as much aim as a baby."

He thrusts the gun at me and nods at a small target he has set up in the corner.

"You try to hit the center, then, if you think it's so

easy," he says, but I shake my head.

"I'm not much for guns. It's not ladylike."

He eyes my torn dress and bloody leg.

"*Ladylike*," he says with a laugh. "Can't see you being too concerned with that."

"You don't know a thing about me."

"Then tell me."

I lean against the railing and cross my legs, realizing I have a fresh audience for my imagination.

"Let's see. Well, I snuck out in the dead of night. It was freezing cold, and—"

"It was cold in Florida?"

"Sometimes," I say. "We lived farther up north."

He nods, as if that's a good enough explanation.

"A train passed behind our house, same time every evening. I could hear it all the way across the swamp. I fought my way through, keeping an eye out for alligators, until I found the tracks. I waited until I could hear it coming, then I started to run, hoping I could catch it before it passed me."

"It must have been going pretty fast."

"It was," I say. "But I made it. Ran with all my might and barely grabbed hold of the last car's handle. You'll *never* guess what I saw inside when I pulled myself in."

"What?" he asks, spellbound.

"A whole group of drifters. Dozens of them. Men,

mostly, and a few women down on their luck. They travel on trains all across the country, you know."

"Wow," George says.

"They were nice. We ate cans of cold food and sang songs all through the night. I wanted to get far away from home, so I stayed with them until we got to—"

What state is above Florida?

"—until we got to another state. I hopped off and set up camp in the woods. Lived there for a time, drinking from streams and eating fruit from the trees, going into town to steal whatever I could. And that's when I saw it—the circus. It had just pulled in and was looking for help, so I told them I'll do any job they want. Shoveling elephant dung. Cleaning the lion cage. I didn't care by that point. Well, the one circus man takes one look at me and says, 'You seem about the right size to be an acrobat, have you ever—'"

"You ain't telling the truth."

"What do you know about anything, George? You ever leave this town in your whole life?"

He looks down his legs.

"So . . . did you join them?"

"For a while. It was good while it lasted. We went from town to town, and they were teaching me lots of things. Said I could be the best acrobat in the world if I kept it up, but I don't much trust circus types. Guess if I knew what was waiting for me after, I might have stuck it out."

"Really? What happened next?"

George's eyes are wide and innocent, and he's caught in my web.

The story moves on to wild tales about my time picketing with the suffragettes, hitchhiking on highways, trips on riverboats, and the convent of nuns I escaped in Virginia. All of it's made up of course, pieces of things I'd read in books or overheard from Mr. Spencer and his friends.

"So, what made you leave your home?" he asks, awestruck by my stories.

I move back in time, back when my mother and father were still alive, and John and I could play in the yard and run our hands through the flowers that lined the edge of the lake. I tell him about our house, the little school I went to, all the perfect days, one after the other. It's still a story, but like most stories, contains a mixture of truth and lie. I tell him my parents died in a fire instead of the flu, and how I ran away before the court could take me to an orphanage.

"What happened to your brother?" he asks, interrupting me.

I pause for effect. "He died, too," I say, stopping my story there. I was getting carried away, and it's best not to tell him too much. "What about you?"

George tells me all about his three younger brothers and his dog and the little orange cat that hunts for birds in the garden. His voice is soft and smooth, and I like listening to it. He tells me about his school and his old teacher who whacks him on the ear whenever he gets an answer wrong, and how much he hates going and wishes he could be a runaway like me. I want to grab him, look him in the eyes, and tell him not to say a stupid thing like that. I want to tell him how lucky he is and how much I'd give to be able to go back to a time when school was all I had to worry about.

We sit in the loose straw for what feels like hours, and maybe it is, because the sun is lower in the sky now. Each day is getting shorter than the last.

George must trust me, because he slides a pile of straw to the side and lifts a board, revealing a secret compartment of his own.

"I have a Hidden Place, too," he says, pulling out a metal box.

"What do you got there?"

"Treasures."

"Well, go on, what's inside?" I ask, and he hesitates to show me even though I can tell he wants to. Finally, he cracks it open and sorts through, holding stuff up piece by piece.

It's just a bunch of old trash, mostly, scraps of paper and rusted metal pieces, funny-shaped rocks and old toys, but he handles each piece like it's the most valuable thing in the world. There's a pack of old, brown playing cards, a rusty pocketknife, some arrowheads, and a leather sack stuffed with fool's gold. George has a story for everything, and I like listening to his adventures by the river and digging through mud under knotted trees.

"Oh! You have to see this!" he says, pulling out a metal tube. "Pa got this in town years ago but says it ain't as good as his lamp, so he gave it to me."

It's shiny, and looks like the handle of a sword, except where the blade would be is a small disc of glass.

"What is it?"

He gives a mischievous grin and aims it into the corner of the loft. His thumb flicks a button and the end of the tube flashes light in a brilliant beam against the dark corner like Mr. Spencer's camera flash, sending shadows of straw against the wall.

"Wow!" I say, and he switches it off. "Hey! Leave it on."

"Can't for more than a few seconds at a time," he explains. "Burns out the bulb. It's only good for quick flashes of light."

"What's it called?"

"*Flash*light," he says, and I laugh real hard at that because I think he's making a joke, but then he points it at my face, switches it on, and bright spots appear in my vision. I fall over, laughing.

It's nice to talk to someone other than John and Mr. Spencer.

"So, where you running away to, anyway?" George asks.

"The Silver Star Society."

He looks at me, mouth open. I shouldn't have told him.

"You ain't really."

I nod.

"Silver Star," he whispers, like he's in a trance.

"You've heard of it?"

"Yes." George leans in, whispers, "They say people can talk to the dead there."

"That so?"

"You shouldn't go," he says.

"Why not? I thought maybe I could ask my parents what they thought of my new life."

I'm teasing him now, but the words get caught in my throat. What *would* my parents think? They'd probably tell me to stop lying, and they'd be pretty sad about how Mr. Spencer treats us, but I know they'd be proud of how I take care of John.

"I'm serious. Don't go."

"Are you scared, George?"

"No. Everyone knows that place is a fake. You're best turning around right now. They trick people into thinking they can talk to ghosts, but there's no such thing. Pastor says it's evil stuff, and anyone that goes there is likely to get possessed by the devil."

"You're not making much sense," I say. "Either it's fake or it's the work of the devil. It can't be both."

"Sure can," he says, and how do I argue with that?

"You don't know what you're talking about, George. No one knows if ghosts are real."

Except I do. They're as real as the cotton and pictures hidden in my suitcase.

"Well, I know it's a Spiritualist place, and Pa says it's full of wicked people. He won't let us go anywhere near it, even takes the longer route to church so we don't see it when we cross the hill, and—"

"Which direction is it?" I ask, ready to end this conversation.

"That way." He points. "Just a couple miles if you go through the woods."

"I better be leaving, then," I say, standing up and crawling down the ladder.

"Don't go," he says, poking his head up to peer down at me through the hole in the loft. "Whatever reason you want to talk to ghosts . . . it ain't worth it."

"I have to."

"Will I see you again?" he asks, and I shake my head, smiling coyly.

"Not unless you visit the Silver Star Society. Ask for Liza if you're brave enough."

"Liza?" he says. "I thought you said your name was Violet."

My face gets hot. I forgot about that. Mr. Spencer was right; I can't keep my stories straight.

"Doesn't matter what my name is," I say, grabbing my suitcase and heading toward the door. "You can't trust anything I say."

"Well, who are you really?"

"Nobody," I say. "I'm dead, George. Just a ghost."

And I leave so fast that he probably thinks I'm telling the truth.

A LITTLE MYSTERY

Treading through the long grass around the farm, I move far enough away from the road that I can hide in the weeds if I have to, and cut into the woods, walking in the direction George pointed.

A small dirt path leads me to a clearing where metal stars and ribbons hang from sticks planted deep in the ground. A stone cross sits in the center, with a star carved at the top and the name ELDRIDGE underneath it in tall letters. The stone is cracked and surrounded by flowers and folded pieces of paper. There are tree stumps around it, sliced at odd angles, pieces of them crumbling away from age and rot. I don't know what this place is but I feel drawn to it. I step forward, and my ears start to buzz.

I trace my fingers along the mossy top of the stone, and shadows move in the woods. The sun has begun to set, and the golden rays cut through the branches of the surrounding trees, leaving little drops of light on the ground.

The shadows seem to circle me. They're closing in, moving across the leaves, flickering with the ribbons, multiplying around me. Suddenly, I don't like how I feel here. I have to move on. It's getting cold, and I want to get inside before it's dark.

When I step out of the woods and crest the hill, I can see straight into the valley. Power lines snake along the woods and down, leading to a giant, white, two-story estate dotted with windows flanked by green wooden shutters. A balcony wraps around the second story, and vines and flowers from potted plants spill out from the railings, hanging so low they almost touch the ground. Long rays of sunlight paint swatches of red on the black slate roof.

Surrounding the property is a neck-high stone wall covered in ivy, and the road leads to a metal gate, which opens into a cobblestone courtyard. There's a large oak tree by the front of the house next to a dirt area to the side where a few horses are tied, and some carriages are pulled up and arranged in neat little rows, and there's even a few black automobiles parked in the grass.

This is where the money *goes*, Mr. Spencer said, and now I'm starting to believe him. This is more of a hotel than a house.

There's movement in the yard. A woman in a yellow dress slinks around, gliding to the back of the building, where there's a cemetery of gray stones poking from the ground. She disappears in the dusk. I get a shiver down my arms and wonder if it was a ghost, but of course that can't be true. Ghosts are made-up things, just like my cotton creations. I know that. I *know* that.

Still, I watch the house, looking for John and Mr. Spencer. All I can see are blurred figures through the windows. When it gets dark enough, lamps are lit in the windows and the whole place seems to tremble in the breeze, like a hard wind could blow it all away.

Horse hooves clop far in the distance.

Now, Liza. Go.

I run down the hill and kneel in a pile of mud, rub it over my arms and face. I set my suitcase in the middle of the road and slink to a ditch by the side, close my eyes and cover my face with my arms.

It's getting colder, and the ground makes it worse. My body hurts, and I start shaking so hard that my teeth rattle around in my head.

How long does it take to freeze to death? I wonder. Except there's no snow or ice and surely you can't freeze to death in autumn, can you?

The night is still, and I can hear sounds from the house, dinner plates clanging, people talking and laughing. The air smells like smoke and frost.

The faint clopping of horse hooves is getting

louder, but they still sound far away, like they're never getting closer, so I stay motionless, waiting, hoping my fingers don't turn blue and snap clean off.

Finally, they're close enough that I can hear the rattling of their straps, and a man yells, "Whoa, there!" The carriage stops in the middle of the road. He sees the suitcase first, grunts in confusion, and then it's not long till his eyes move over to me in the ditch.

"Whoa," he says again.

His boots slap against the ground, and then his hands are on my shoulders, pulling me up. A woman's voice calls out from the carriage, "Excuse me? Why did we stop? What's wrong?"

"There's a little girl in the ditch," the driver answers.

"Oh, heavens!" the woman says.

He presses the back of his hand to my neck. "Looks half dead."

A moan escapes my lips and I collapse into him. His arms are warm, and I start shivering again and then I can't stop. He puts me on his seat in the back of the carriage and whips at the reins, driving toward the house.

"Don't go *there*," the woman whispers.

"There isn't much choice. She needs help now."

The driver stops at the gate, calling out, "Hello!

Is someone there?" and a Black man with a mustache runs out and opens it.

We pass through into the courtyard, and I feel light-headed, like the air is thinner in this place. Different, somehow. A chill starts at my neck and works down my arms and legs. It must all be in my mind. It was so cold on that road, and I'm tired from traveling all day.

Suddenly, there's a swarm of people around me, running from the house and surrounding the carriage.

A big woman with gray hair clipped in a bun on top of her head pulls me from the seat and sets me on the ground. She pries open my eyes and stares into them.

"Is she all right?" the driver asks.

"She's alive," the woman says. "Looks to be in a rough state."

I give another moan, louder this time, but it starts a cough that I can hardly stop, and my lungs burn from the cold air.

"Found her by the side of the road," the driver says, hat in his hands. He looks at the house and all the people in the yard, no doubt having heard tales of the people here. "She only had this with her."

He lays my suitcase down beside me and steps back, as if leaving a piece of meat to a rabid dog.

Suddenly, he seems to have a change of heart.

"Actually, if she seems well enough, I can take her to the next town. There's a doctor there that can—"

"That will be all right. Thank you for your help," the gray-haired lady says. The driver returns to the cab and hops back in, racing away from the place like that rabid dog might break free and give chase.

The woman in the yellow dress, the same one I saw walking around the gravestones, comes and feels my hands.

"Ice cold," she says. "I'll boil a bath."

"Thank you, Margaret," the gray-haired lady says. She stares into my eyes. "I was expecting you, darling, and here you are, right on time. Tell me your name."

I don't say anything yet, still pretending to be too weak to speak. Stories are so important at the beginning. There's an awful lot you can get wrong.

She scoops me up and carries me toward the front door, where I see Mr. Spencer leaning against a pole on the porch, smoking a pipe. John sits beside him, his hands folded in his lap and his hair neatly combed to the side. A small, orange corgi sits beside him, panting heavily. The dog whines at me as I pass by, and John seems to look right through me, like I'm not even there.

Good, John, I think. *Keep pretending.*

The crowd follows us back into the warmth of the

house, and the lady sets me down in a room with a fireplace. It's so warm that I nearly giggle with joy.

"Ms. Eldridge, should I call the police?" the man with the mustache asks. His voice is deep and commanding, but the way he asks tells me he's not in charge here.

Eldridge. The same last name that I saw on the stone in the woods.

"That won't be necessary, Charles," Ms. Eldridge says, clucking her tongue. "They'd love any reason to poke their noses around, and I won't give them a chance without cause."

Charles is wearing a blue suit, a bit too big for his thin body, but he's handsome in it. His hair is neatly cut, peppered with gray, and he wears little round glasses that reflect the light of the fire. Charles slides my suitcase over and she opens it, sorts through my clothes and pulls out a pair of wool pajamas.

"Filthy old things, but this looks warmer. Take it back to Margaret."

"Any name on the handle?" Charles asks.

"Nothing," she says, sorting through my clothes and tossing a blue dress on a chair. Luckily, she doesn't dig too deep. "She's a little mystery, isn't she? Just a few ratty dresses and socks. Poor thing looks like she's running from something."

"We really should call the police, ma'am."

"Charles!" Ms. Eldridge says, and when she stands, I can see what an imposing figure she is; tall and thick, with rough hands that look like they've done a good deal of hard work. "I will not tell you again."

Charles slinks off, holding my pajamas in his hands.

Soon, Margaret reappears and tells Ms. Eldridge that the water is boiled, and the two women pull me away from the fire and lead me through the house.

I pass a crowded room and see Mr. Spencer has moved inside to the parlor, legs crossed, fingers pulling invisible strings in the air, telling stories that I know are full of lies. John sits on the floor beside him, a smile on his lips as he pats the small dog's head.

The house seems even larger inside, constructed of long hallways with creaky, uneven floors, and we pass gas lamps on the walls that flicker with our movement.

"You'll bathe back here," Margaret says, pointing at a room filled with people.

Shocked, I almost open my mouth to protest, but when I get closer, the people fade, morphing into mere shadows cast by curtains and furniture. Tricks of the light—and now I see that it's just me and the woman, alone. My heart beats faster at the surprise. I *swear* I saw eyes looking at me, I was sure they were—

No. *No.* I blink and take in the room again. It's attached to the back of the house. It was probably a porch once, but now it has solid white walls and large windows on three sides. There's a bath in the center, surrounded by an overhanging circular curtain. The room is warm and hazy with steam, and I slip inside the curtain and peel off my dress, stepping into the hot water.

I melt like ice.

IF YOU BELIEVE

The woman in the yellow dress tells me her name is Margaret Price, but I only half listen to her as I let the water bubble in my ears. A small lamp flickers, casting more shadows around the room, and now that I'm warm, I realize how silly I was to think they were anything different. Margaret has draped my pajamas over the curtain rod, and I can see her silhouette through the curtain, distorted by the folds in the fabric.

"Do you know where you are?" she asks.

I don't answer.

"This is the Silver Star Society. When explorers set sail on the oceans, they used the stars to guide them to the new world. Here, it's her guiding light that leads us to the spirits, with the help of Ms. Eldridge."

I sit up in the tub and look through a crack in the curtain. Margaret's moved to a chair and leans over. She's beautiful in the soft light, and her eyes stare into mine.

"Long ago, a woman named Annabelle Eldridge lived here. She died when her granddaughter was just a young girl. That's the age when the soul is most open to spirits, and the girl heard her grandmother speaking from the other side—could even see her some nights, walking in the valley and up into the woods. Her grandmother's spirit was still latched to her, but the girl helped usher it over, to the place where she belonged, and has been able to speak to her ever since."

I think of that gray-haired lady in the hall, how she looked in my eyes and told me she was expecting me. I hold back a smile. The story is even sillier than Mr. Spencer's, their lie so simple.

"I know. It all must sound strange, but it's true. Ms. Eldridge is my cousin. She's the one that suggested I come here after . . ." Her voice trails off.

I know what she's about to say. I know the look people have when they're about to tell a sad story. I slide back into the water, try to keep a blank look on my face. I think of that strange place I passed earlier, the stone cross and the metal stars, the ribbons hanging from sticks and the folded notes.

"We're at a thin place between the worlds of the living and the spirits here. That's what makes it so exciting. You'll see. Have you ever lost someone close to you?"

Tears form in the corners of her eyes. I bite my cheek so I don't cry too.

"Of course, you have. Why else would you be here, little one? Will you tell me your story?"

I turn my head, wishing she would leave me alone to soak the cold away.

"No? I will tell you mine, then. My husband passed three years ago. We don't use the word *died* here," she says, looking out toward the cemetery. "I still talk to him often."

You don't, I think, but to tell her that would be cruel.

"No one's ever really gone, you see. They are all around us. Some days I feel that I could hold my breath and hop over, just for a time, and then hop right back. Did you notice it when you came here?"

I shake my head, even though I remember the chill that passed through me as I entered the gates. But that was only because I was cold, and nothing more.

"Some people feel it more strongly than others. Through Ms. Eldridge and Annabelle, you can communicate with anyone if you believe."

If you believe. There they are. Three words that make everything else a lie. Three sneaky words that make it easy to trick people out of their money.

"Anyway, you must be hungry." She leaves a towel for me and exits the room, saying, "Come to the dining room when you're dressed. I'll get a plate of food ready."

I don't want to get out of the warm tub, but my stomach rumbles at the thought of eating. I dry off, step into my pajamas, and pat down my hair, but it's a half-hearted attempt. The soggy strands whip across my back as I move through the halls, lured to the smell of dinner.

The conversation stops when I step into the dining room. There's still a half dozen people seated around the table, holding little saucers and cups of coffee. Their clothes look expensive, suits and dresses, and I feel out of place in my pajamas. There's no time for me to feel shy, because Margaret appears beside me with a plate of hot food and motions to a chair. It's roast beef with gravy and a big helping of mashed potatoes next to a side of boiled carrots. I haven't had a meal like this in years, back when father was out working and mother would cook all afternoon. The smell of the gravy takes me back there—I can almost see Mother in the kitchen wearing her blue apron, stirring the pot, singing under her breath. I grab a spoon like a feral child and start shoveling, even though I know I should slow down. It's bad to eat this fast on an empty stomach.

John's sitting across the table from me with his hands folded on his lap, and a strand of hair sticks up at his cowlick. I want to reach across the table and push it down.

He smiles at me, and I try not to smile back.

Mr. Spencer's sprawled in his seat, his arm draped over the back with his legs crossed and the tip of his shoe tapping the underside of the table. He watches me eat.

"What horrible manners," he says. "She chews like a cow."

I don't know if the disgust is part of his act or if that's the truth spilling out on account of his drinking, but I don't pay it any mind. The food is too good to care. I shovel it into my mouth, accidentally dropping a piece on the floor. The dog runs beside me and gobbles it up, then nuzzles its head against my leg.

"I see you've met Fox," Ms. Eldridge says. "If you feed her, she'll be your friend forever."

"Fox is a good name for her," I say.

She has a white stripe between her eyes and down her nose, and her ears stick up in little triangles. She looks at me, panting, begging me to drop another piece.

"She's a stray too. Came to us one day, and never left."

"She seems happy."

"We take good care of her. Now leave the girl

alone, Fox. The poor little thing likely hasn't eaten in days," Ms. Eldridge says, and the dog obeys.

Sitting here, Ms. Eldridge looks like the queen of a kingdom. Her presence engulfs the room. Her gray hair is streaked with patches that are nearly white, and the whole thing is tied up in a bun with a glass butterfly clip. She wears a black dress with a lace collar around her neck, and there are large silver rings on most of her fingers that clank on her cup as she sips her water.

"So where are you from, girl?" Mr. Spencer asks, knocking his knuckles on the table to signal that he doesn't want an answer.

"Florida," I whisper, and he scowls at me.

"Poor thing is a runaway by the looks of it," Ms. Eldridge says. "It's good fortune that she found us."

"What will we do with her?" Mr. Spencer asks. He's only been here a few hours and he's already acting like the house is his.

"I've been considering my options. I could send her into town tomorrow, but questions will follow. Something tells me that for now, she is right where she needs to be."

Mr. Spencer nods, pleased by this answer. "When I leave, I can take her with me. Could use the company, and if she causes any trouble, I'll leave her with the proper authorities."

"I don't think that will be necessary, but thank you for the kind and generous offer," Ms. Eldridge says, with a tone that seems to mean the opposite of her words. She stares at me and I look away.

I hate that they're talking about me like I'm not here, but none of it matters. I don't care where I go as long as John is with me. Mr. Spencer gives me a look that tells me her reaction has surprised him, but he masks it well and leans back in his chair.

"More guests arriving tomorrow, then?" he asks.

"Indeed," Ms. Eldridge says. "Our numbers ebb and flow, some days more than others. People are drawn by word of new people such as yourself on the premises. Tomorrow night, every bed will be claimed."

Mr. Spencer's eyes flash, calculating the riches soon to come.

"How wonderful," he says, standing to leave. "With that, I will retire for the evening. Good night to you all."

"You must understand my hesitation in inviting you to this place," Ms. Eldridge says. Mr. Spencer freezes, caught between the chair and the door, and an uncomfortable chill crosses the room. No one pays me any mind now, which is fine, because it means no one is watching me eat. "There are some that believe the whole business of spiritual photography is a fake.

Mr. Mumler was exposed. The Ackerman brothers proved it time and time again, duplicating the results with tricks of exposures and developing. It's so hard to tell the frauds from the faithful, and some have said that we lessen the credibility of the Silver Star Society by having you here."

Others at the table nod, like they were all thinking the same thing and Ms. Eldridge was the only one who could say it.

"*Fraud?*" Mr. Spencer asks, holding his hand against his chest and doing a good impression of being offended. "You know as well as I, that what is not understood is often called a trick. If you ask me to describe how the spirit world works, I am sorry to say that I cannot. Those explanations would be better left to people like *you*."

"Don't talk to her like that!" Charles says, standing, and Ms. Eldridge waves him off.

"He meant no offense, I'm sure."

Mr. Spencer is quietly seething with anger. He can hide it from the others, but not from me.

"Simply because there's no explanation does not mean that I am a fraud. Aren't there magicians that can re-create what you do, too?"

Ms. Eldridge nods, a slight smile on her lips. She's enjoying this, even if no one else in the room is.

"I'll remind you that I let your man Charles fully

examine my camera upon arrival. Did you find anything out of the ordinary?"

Charles shakes his head. "No, sir."

"And I let Charles purchase the photographic plates for tomorrow's portraits. He has them guarded in his room to ensure that no trickery is afoot." He glances at me to make sure I heard him. "I will never so much as touch them. He will slide them in my camera, take them out, and develop the images himself. If I am a con man, surely I would not allow these indignities. Unless of course, you believe Charles is working with me."

There's nervous laughter, and Ms. Eldridge talks over it.

"These precautions are only because my reputation is on the line. I'm sure you understand."

"Tomorrow you'll see the truth, and I'll accept no more accusations." Mr. Spencer leaves and John looks at me before pulling himself up from the table and walking out of the room.

"I think I may have offended him," Ms. Eldridge says, sipping from her glass with a twinkle in her eye.

"Why did you invite him here?" Charles asks. "He's as crooked a man as I've ever seen."

"Curiosity at first, but now I think there may be more to it than that," she says, and then turns to me and smiles. "You had quite an appetite, young lady. Was everything to your liking?"

I nod and try not to look at her eyes.

"Time for bed, then. Come now."

Ms. Eldridge takes me by the hand and leads me up the stairs to a long hallway with a half dozen doors on the right side. The house is a mixture of old and new. There are light bulbs mounted in the ceiling, as well as gold wall sconces holding flickering candles. The walls are covered in faded green wallpaper, and there are pictures of angels and lambs hanging along them. I pay careful attention to the floorboards, marking in my mind which ones creak and which are silent. We turn left, walking along the back side of the house, and there are even more doors here. This must be the biggest house in the world. I'll need to plan ahead if I want to find where Charles sleeps.

"We have some empty rooms until more guests arrive tomorrow. You may stay here tonight."

She opens the door to a small room. My suitcase is already inside, next to a high blue bed with a wooden frame. There's a rug and bookshelf, and a painting of a farmer in a field with fiery clouds hanging above. A window looks out to the woods, and an oil lamp flickers on the ledge.

I step inside and rub my fingers on the bed's fabric.

A chill goes up my arm. It's been so long since I've slept in a proper bed, and I'm scared that Mr. Spencer will take it away from me. But he won't. He *can't*. Not here. Not where he can't admit to knowing me.

Ms. Eldridge kneels and looks me in the eyes, says, "I know you've come here for help. I don't know if I'm strong enough, but I'll try."

There's that stare again, like she's seeing through me, to things happening in my mind. I don't answer, and she turns and walks down the hall without looking back.

THE GHOST IN THE NIGHT

In the bed, I wrap the blankets around me like a cocoon and drift in and out of sleep for a few hours until I hear footsteps in the hall. The guests are turning in for the night, which means my work is about to begin. First, I need to find out which room belongs to Charles.

I creep out of my room and tiptoe down the hallway until I reach a corner. On the other side is a grandfather clock. Its hands tell me it's half past eleven, and I press my back against the wall beside it. The ticking of the pendulum seems to beat with the rhythm of my heart. Small wooden tables covered with lamps and decorations line the hallway. There's a metal vase on one, and I can see a reflection of the stairs from around the corner. Guests of the Society pass by, nodding at me, saying good night, and I wait, watching the polished silver until I see Charles's head rise from the steps. He's holding a book in one hand and a candle in the other. The light glows against his dark skin, and he stumbles down the hall, absorbed in his reading, not looking where he's going until he reaches a familiar spot. He turns into his room and—

Click. I capture the door in my memory.

That's where the camera supplies are, and that's where I'll need to go.

For now, I return to my room and lie in bed, forcing myself not to drift off. The grandfather clock doesn't chime at night, so I wait an hour, maybe two, until the house is quiet.

Now is the time.

I slink back into the hallway, but it's silent now, except for the wind in the trees outside, and in my stocking feet, I am as soft as the passing breeze. Each floorboard is different, but I know them now. They're familiar friends. I start each step with my big toe, then follow with the ball of my foot, then the heel. I test each board before setting my full weight down, moving in slow motion. Blood pounds in my ears.

When Charles's door is in reach, I press my ear against it and listen to his soft breathing. I turn the knob and lean in. He's sprawled on his stomach, and the moon shines through the window and casts a soft light on the side of his face.

His bedroom is the same shape as mine, but a bit smaller, and it's clear he's lived here for a while and doesn't keep it as clean as the guest rooms. The dust makes my nose itch and I close my eyes, breathe in, breathe out, trying not to sneeze. There's a pile of clothes stacked on a chair and a dresser under the window. A folded paper bag sits beside it. It's just the right size, and I slink forward, timing each step to Charles's snores. What will I do if he wakes up and sees me? He'd tell Ms. Eldridge and then everything would be ruined. It's hard to believe your whole life can hinge around one little moment. I look at the heavy bronze lamp in the corner. I'd have to—

No. No, I couldn't hurt him. Best not to think of those things.

My hand curls around the bag and I unfold it, each tiny sound seeming as loud as thunder. Finally, it's open wide enough that I can peek in.

A pocketknife. A hardback book and a tortoiseshell comb. A small, framed photograph of Margaret. Some pennies and a lone nickel. *Nothing's ever easy.*

I open the top drawer and shuffle through his clothes, letting my hands feel for shapes.

Not here.

The next drawer down reveals similar results, same with the one below it and the next, but then in the final drawer, under a pile of clothes, I feel a box wrapped in paper. I know what it is from the touch. I pull it out, softly, and move to the door. Charles stops snoring and I freeze in place, but then he changes positions, and the soft snores continue.

I return to my room, faster now, following the path of silent boards. I reach the bend in the hallway and check the reflection in the silver vase. The hall is empty.

Inside my room, I open the suitcase and slide my fingers over the false bottom, removing the supplies from my Hidden Place to do my work.

I think back to years ago, before I ever doctored a photograph, when we first started living with Mr. Spencer.

It was a warm spring night, not at all like today. The windows in our rented room were open, crickets were singing, and the air smelled like sweet flowers.

"Look at this," Mr. Spencer said. He pulled an image from a box and slid a picture of a woman over to me.

"This is Mrs. Turner. Died last month in childbirth. Her husband owns a business in town. I think there may be some money for us if we're smart."

"What do you mean?" I whispered.

He sat across the table from me and pulled a knife out of his shirt pocket. He smiled. I never saw him smile before, and there was something unsettling about how it looked on his face.

"What do you say we give them one last picture?"

He started to cut, tracing around her hair, her

ears, her jaw. His hand was shaking hard that day, and his work was unsteady and rough. He slipped, making a long gash down the side of the woman's dress.

"Let me try," I said, and he slid the knife and paper over to me as if that had been his plan all along. He pulled out his pipe and a bag of tobacco and filled the bowl, tamping it down with his pinkie.

I cut around Mrs. Turner's face, fixing the jagged edges left over from Mr. Spencer's work until I could lick the tip of my finger and press it to the image, lift it up and away.

"Here."

"Beautiful," he said, taking her head and laying it on a thick wooden board that had been painted black. "Well?"

"What are we making?" I asked, still not understanding.

"A ghost," Mr. Spencer said.

John watched from the corner. He came beside me, leaning forward so he could see above the table.

"Ain't look like no ghost," John said.

"No, it *doesn't* look right," I said. He hadn't been in school for months at that point, and he was picking up bad habits from Mr. Spencer's friends.

"Well then, what do you suggest?" Mr. Spencer asked.

I smiled devilishly at John, too caught up in creation to think through the harm. "Mr. Spencer, you got any cotton?"

"What are you doing?" John whispered in my ear, but I pushed him away.

Mr. Spencer stood and returned with a mason jar half full of cotton balls, and I pulled one out and started ripping it apart between my hands, twisting the strands. I laid it beneath the head like the stick of a lollipop.

"Ah," Mr. Spencer said.

"Needs to wrap around it more," John said. "Like she's floating."

I moved the pieces around, shaping the cotton around her hair, creating the rough shape of her body, fading away to the ground and ending in a twirl of white.

"They call that ectoplasm," Mr. Spencer said, leaning back in his chair and grinning. He lit a match, sucked deeply on his pipe, and blew out smoke, the fine white cloud circling his head. "Say it's *spiritual energy*."

"Who says?" I asked.

"Spiritualists."

That was the first time I ever heard that word. "Who are they?"

"Fools who will believe they can talk to the dead,

and will pay a good amount to be lied to. I happen to know Mr. Turner is a believer."

He twisted the knob on the lantern and the light dimmed. My eyes adjusted to the faint light from the moon.

"Do you know what this is?" he asked, opening a box and holding up a square of glass.

I shake my head.

"This is a photographic *plate*," he said, tracing his fingers along the edge. "It's coated with chemicals. When the camera lens focuses light on the surface, it bakes it into the glass. Watch."

Mr. Spencer slid the plate into the camera and turned the knob again, so the flame danced in the lantern. He propped the board with my picture and cotton creation against the wall and arranged the lantern to the side, just enough to make the whole thing glow.

He framed it in the camera and twisted the lens.

"When things are out of focus, people see what they want," he said.

Click.

He held out his fingers, counting out how long the shutter was open, collecting a hint of light, just enough to leave faint shapes on the photographic plate.

"What's he doing?" John asked.

"Come. I'll take your portrait," Mr. Spencer said.

"John too? I'd like one of us together," I asked.

He growled and waved at us to follow him to a room with a curtain draped across the wall as a backdrop, and he arranged the chair and placed the tripod in front of me.

"Sit," he said, and I obeyed. I always obeyed, never questioned. John sat close to me.

Mr. Spencer removed a Victor flashlamp from a box. It was metal and shaped like a T. A wire connected it to the camera's shutter. He unscrewed a little glass bottle full of flash powder and poured a measured amount into a trough at the top. He aimed the camera at us, the glass lens looking like the single black eye of a cyclops, then held up his hand and—

Click.

The shutter opened and an electric current raced through a wire, ignited the powder in the flash and—

Boom!

Smoke and a shower of sparks filled the room for a moment, but the smell of burning chemicals was strong and lingered.

Mr. Spencer retreated to his darkroom, worked on the plates, mixed chemicals in trays, and developed the image. Later, he emerged with a paper in his hand. It was an image of me and John, with the spirit of Mrs. Turner seemingly wrapped around our shoulders.

"It's a double exposure," he explained. "Like magic."

I stared in awe at what I had created. With the face and cotton out of focus, my imagination filled in the rest, turning the blurred shapes into familiar figures. Even though I knew the face belonged to Mrs. Turner, when I squinted, it almost looked like our mother.

When things are out of focus, people see what they want.

It took us a few weeks to figure out how much flash powder to use for the portrait and how long the exposure of the face on the black-painted board should be, but I've still kept that photo with me ever since. It's the only picture I have of me and John since our parents died, a reminder of how this started, how Mr. Spencer used my creation to create another double exposure, then called on Mr. Turner the next day and took his picture. He charged him five times the normal fee for him to see his wife's spirit. Word spread quickly and so did our business. Our new life was created, traveling from place to place, stealing what we could and lying when it suited us, until we ended up here.

Tonight is another one of those little moments that can change everything. If I don't change the plates, nothing else will matter. I get to work, hoping I can finish in time to sleep. There's a book of matches on the windowsill and I light the lantern and uncurl the stolen package from Charles's room. Inside is a box of ten photographic plates, and I scrape off the piece of tape that seals it and place it on my bed frame.

I flip through my stack of photos, hunting for bland faces, a mixture of men and women, ones that could pass as anyone. No kids, not yet anyway, not when we don't know who we will be photographing. Keep it safe. Everyone's lost an adult.

This one's good. And this one. No, not that one. The birthmark on her face is too obvious. This one's perfect. This one. Yes, this one too.

The stack of pictures grows, and when I have enough, I start to cut, creating ghosts, moving fast.

There's a sound in the hall and a thumping down the stairs. I freeze, waiting to pounce on my work if someone enters my room.

Outside, a shadow moves across the lawn, entering the outhouse. Steam rises from the door.

I blow out the lantern, wait till they're back inside to relight it and then move it to my bed and prop up the black-painted board, arranging the paper ghosts on its surface. The glass plates slide smoothly into my camera and I extend the bellows, frame the picture in front of the lens, twist the lens just slightly out of focus, hold in my breath, and—

Click.

A faint exposure, hardly visible, then on to the next one, then the next, allowing the shutter to stay open long enough to gather up the faint echoes of light.

Hours pass, and I continue working until all the photographic plates have been used, then leave drops of candle wax on the corner of each of the plates— one drop for the women and two for the men—a sign Mr. Spencer taught me. Then I pull the tape from my bed frame and reseal it, slide it back into the bag and curl down the edges, just like I found it.

Outside, the bottom of the sky has changed from dark black to a faint blue. My heart beats fast. I place my tools in my Hidden Place and camera on top, place the top back on and cover it with clothes.

The hall is silent now and I sneak back to Charles's room and crack open the door. He's still asleep, thank goodness, so I move directly to the bottom drawer and put the package back under his clothes.

I was never there.

Tiptoeing back down the hall, I stop in front of the silver vase. In the reflection, a shape moves at the end of the hall—the silhouette of a woman. It almost looks like two white eyes staring at me, beneath a nest of cotton-colored hair. A draft blows across my arm, and I don't move. Don't breathe.

The reflection is distorted, but the woman is too small to be Ms. Eldridge. Could it be Margaret? Or someone else?

I step forward, and before my eyes the shadows bleed into the wall. I blink in disbelief, and the shape seems to vanish. Yesterday, spots appeared in my vision when George shone his flashlight in my eyes. Things can appear that aren't really there.

Back in my room, I jump into bed and pull the blankets over my head.

Deep in the house, I can hear John coughing, a soft, wet rattle that echoes in my head.

THE SILVER STAR SOCIETY

The morning sun is harsh through the frosted window, and the sky is on fire, just like the painting on my wall. I don't know how long I've slept, but my body is still sore from yesterday's journey and working late into the night, and the bed is so soft and warm.

Sounds come from outside, talking and laughing, and horse hooves tap against stone. The big front door opens and closes, opens and closes, and the house is filled with conversation.

Charles talks in the hallway outside my room. I recognize his voice. It's a low rumble, and Margaret answers, then the door opens a crack and I peek through my eyelashes to see her.

"Is she asleep?" Charles asks.

She smiles, steps forward, and touches my shoulder.

"Faking it, I suspect."

In the morning light, Margaret looks like a porcelain doll that's come to life. It seems impossible that she is related to Ms. Eldridge. Today, her dress is blue, and her hair flows to the side in big swoops that look like waterfalls, crashing over the smooth rocks of her shoulders.

She sticks out a toe and slides the suitcase closer to me and for a moment I panic, thinking she might open it and find my Hidden Place.

"Get some clothes on, dear," she says, and leaves the room.

I pull on a faded dress and slip on my shoes, looking out the window to see people gathered in the yard. They stand by the stone wall and face the sun with their hands shielding their eyes.

"Come," Margaret says as I open the door. "It's time for breakfast."

She grabs my hand and leads me down the hall. This time I step without care, letting the boards squeal under my feet.

Charles follows us, past his bedroom door and down the stairs, where the main rooms of the house are full of guests. Some are standing and others are sitting in chairs, talking to each other, holding back tears as they tell stories of the people they've lost. There's laughter, too, as memories are shared.

Margaret leads me to a table. Most people have already eaten breakfast, because the white tablecloth is stained with grease and coffee.

"One more plate!" Margaret yells, and from the kitchen, a man responds with, "We're just cleaning up."

"You can scrounge up some more," Margaret says, and blends into the swarm of people around us.

Soon, a plate appears. Eggs, potatoes, and a few slices of ham glazed in a warm gravy. I look around the room until I see a small figure glide through the crowd, cowlick quivering like a bug's antenna.

John.

Charles sits next to me and tucks a napkin into his shirt.

"I won't make you eat alone," he says, snapping his fingers at the kitchen staff for another plate. "Didn't have time yet this morning, but it all smells so good."

When it arrives, he scoops out small portions, arranging them in a circle around his plate so they don't touch, and then cutting up the meat into perfect little cubes.

"Has anyone told you about this place?" he asks.

"Not really," I mumble, not letting on what I already know. "Margaret told me about Annabelle."

Charles smiles. "Ah, our own guiding star. Well, that's a good start."

Charles divides the eggs on his plate and lays his

knife in the middle. He points to the left side.

"These eggs are us," he says, and then points to the eggs on the other side. "And these are the spirits of the people who passed over to the spirit world."

A man moves behind us and laughs. "They don't look different to me."

"Yes, sir, that's true. And in a way, it's the point I'm trying to make."

Charles is nothing if not polite. He taps the knife with his finger.

"When you die, you pass through this wall, a barrier that separates the living from the spirits."

Charles picks up a piece of egg from the living side of the plate and moves it across.

"Just like that," he says. "And it's there that you live for all eternity, in Summerland, separated from the living."

He places an egg in the middle of the plate, right under the knife.

"There are people, however, who are born with a gift. They can speak through the wall to people on the other side. They are called *mediums*."

I take a bite of my eggs and he smiles. He seems kinder than he did last night, but maybe he has an act too. I need to be careful.

"Like this knife, the wall between us has thick and thin parts."

He points his index finger to the part of the knife where the blade meets the handle.

"This house sits on a spot where the wall is exceptionally thin. Do you understand what that means?" Charles leans in close and whispers, "It's all right if you don't believe. Some days, I'm not sure I do, either."

Ms. Eldridge appears in the room, and her eyes lock with mine.

"Ah, my girl, you look much better today!" she says. "I trust you slept well?"

Without waiting for me to answer, she wraps her hands around my shoulders and calls out, "Attention!"

The room falls silent. Every head turns to us.

"I am so honored to have each of you here today, though I am under no illusions as to *why* you are. Loss is the common thread that runs between us. We are in a special place now. Did you feel it when you entered?"

Soft murmurs fill the room. Mr. Spencer smiles in the corner.

"Science doesn't understand how this is possible. Many doubt our truth. They say we are foolish at best and liars at worst."

I feel she's talking directly to Mr. Spencer, but she continues on, releasing her grip on me and moving through the room. She looks up to the ceiling and closes her eyes, and in this light she is almost beautiful, too, like a monument carved in stone.

"There are things we hold in our hearts—small flames of truth that we must protect from the never-ending breeze of disbelief. If we can protect our fire, guard it from those forces, no one can deceive us."

She turns to the crowd and extends her arms.

"Séances will be held regularly in the assembly hall and in the field, and Margaret's class on astral projection will be held tomorrow by the large tree. This week, we're honored to be joined by some special guests. Wilma Van Heusen is here to demonstrate the art of spiritual paintings, and Madam Crimson has her spirit trumpets in the parlor. And of course, Thomas Spencer, the infamous spirit photographer, will be set up in the basement. Schedules have been posted around the grounds."

"Follow me," Charles says, reaching for my hand. "I could use a helper today."

He leads me through the house while Ms. Eldridge's voice echoes through the halls with more instructions. We travel a different path than last night. The house is full of narrow stairways and hidden compartments lined with slatted boards that let you stand in the shadows and see right through, and Charles knows all the secret passageways in the house, the small doors that open up to tight halls that lead out to unexpected places.

"This house used to be part of the Underground Railroad," he says. "Have you heard of that?"

I nod. Father told me and John about it after we heard mention of it in a book and thought it must be trains that traveled in tunnels under the earth.

"I thought so. You seem like a girl with smarts. That's how my grandfather got up north by way of the Carolinas. Always wondered if he may have passed through here."

Then why don't you have Ms. Eldridge ask Annabelle? I think, but hold the words back. No use starting arguments.

We pass a prayer group gathered in a small sitting room, and take a route through the kitchen, then he leads me to the dining room and to the stairs.

"I don't know your name," Charles says, as if realizing it for the first time.

I feel like I owe him something after what I did to the camera supplies he was guarding last night. "Liza," I say, deciding to go with my real name so I don't need to keep my story straight.

"Pleased to meet you, Liza," he says. "It's a pretty name. I'm Charles Branch."

Up the stairs, we follow the hall to his room and

he opens the door. I don't go in, trying not to look inside in the daylight, ashamed at how familiar I am with the contents of his dresser.

"Today should be interesting," he says. "Ms. Eldridge fancies herself a skeptic, too, despite what you may think. Physical mediumship—that is, people who use props to communicate, are often nothing more than failed tricksters. We've had our share of frauds come through these doors, and she always does her best to catch them in their lies. She thinks of it as her *service* to the Spiritualist community. She's destroyed a good many careers, but has a habit of missing the easy signs." Charles pulls the brown paper bag out of his bottom drawer and raps it with his knuckles. "Which is why we're not letting this leave our sight."

I keep my face blank, try not to show any emotion, and follow him back downstairs where a crowd has gathered in the parlor. Dark curtains cover the windows, blocking out all the light, and people sit in a circle around a large woman. This must be Madam Crimson. She has dark hair and a giant mole on her cheek. She wears a red silk hat with tiny gold tassels dangling from the side, and her accent sounds like it comes from a faraway country, with a bit of New York. Still, it's soothing, somehow, the way the words rise and fall like music.

"Are you here, spirits?" she asks.

A tapping sound comes, seemingly out of nowhere. It gets louder and louder, shaking the pictures on the walls.

"Can you hear them? They've come!"

She places a long, cone-shaped trumpet on the table and stands, walking behind the cabinet she's brought with her, painted with bright colors and animals.

"I will not touch this trumpet again. I will not go near it."

The tapping continues, and a soft murmur comes from the cabinet.

"The spirits are here, whispering around us!"

The crowd of people look around, hoping to see one for themselves. A woman begins to weep.

"Speak into the trumpet, spirits! Let them hear you!"

A strange sound comes from the trumpet, like air squeezing from a balloon. I can't figure out how she's doing it.

Margaret stands by the entrance of the room, watching the trumpet closely.

"Listen!" Madam Crimson shrieks, and her jewelry jingles as she begins to dance. Her bulky body moves and shakes, and the strange trumpet sounds continue. *Phhhheeeeeee phhhheeeeeee phhhheeeeeee. I am here.*

John appears in the hallway. He starts to smile, holding back a laugh, and it's all I can do not to join him.

Phhhheeeeee. I am so happy on the other side.

The voice is small and high-pitched, like a child's, and a man stands and says, "Samuel, is that you?"

The room breaks into commotion, and Charles taps me on the arm, pointing to the door. I don't know if he saw me looking at John, so I follow him, head down, reminding myself to be careful.

We walk down wooden steps to a large dirt-floor basement with stone walls. It's dark, with small windows along the ceiling, spaced in between the beams. The basement is only partially underground. The back wall opens outside to the cemetery, and there are two double doors with a beam across them. On the right side of the basement is a series of doors that must lead to smaller storage rooms, and on the left are shelves full of tools and scraps of wood.

A stool sits in the middle of the large room. There's a folded black blanket on top and Charles takes it, stands on the stool, and hammers it into the beam.

"Have you ever had your picture taken?" he asks, and I lie and shake my head.

"Sit here," he instructs, moving the stool in front of the blanket. He closes one eye, putting me in position, marking a spot. He draws a line in the dirt with his toe and then goes into a corner room, returning with a heavy wooden tripod and placing it on the mark.

"Click," he says, mimicking the sound of a camera, and laughs. "I'm just pretending. The plates are expensive so we can't use them yet. But I suspect we'll have extra ones soon, once Mr. Spencer is proven to be a liar and chased from this place."

Not likely, I think, and smile back at him.

PART TWO

LIGHT & SHADOWS

THE TEST

The basement door opens, and Mr. Spencer's boots appear on the steps, his camera cradled in his arms. Others follow him down, watching as he circles the room, breathes in the dusty air, measures the position of the stool from the tripod. He spins the stool around and moves the tripod back a few inches, not because the position was wrong, but because Charles put it there.

Charles lifts the beam to the double doors that lead outside and opens them, letting the sunlight pour inside the room, giving a warm glow to the wooden walls. Shadows move across the room, bending around the surfaces.

Mr. Spencer paces, talking to the guests, and Charles watches his every move, looking for trickery. He doesn't suspect that the work is already done. When the basement is full, Mr. Spencer pulls the T-shaped flash from his case and holds it to his chest.

He begins his speech, working through his well-rehearsed lie.

"You may ask how I was introduced to Spiritualism. The truth is, it wasn't something I sought out. It came to me. I was a simple photographer, and quickly found that there was something else to my photos. Something *spiritual*," Mr. Spencer says, lowering his head like he's deep in thought. He's polished today, steady, at his very best.

"Strange wisps and shadows appeared, hovering above the bodies. I thought they were mistakes at first. Cracks in the lens. Leaks of light. What else could it be? I sought wisdom from leading Spiritualists who all told me the same thing: It was the ghosts of those who had passed over, staying with those who cared about them."

The crowd listens, unable to look away from him. Sometimes, once Mr. Spencer gets talking, I forget everything he says is a lie. I think if I listened long enough, maybe I'd even start to believe him, even knowing what I did to the photographic plates last night.

He nods to the camera.

"I've come to learn that it is not the tools I use—*it's me*. The spirits are drawn to *me* like moths to a flame. The camera doesn't matter. Many feel what I'm about to do is a cheap trick, not worthy of a place like this. I have made every effort to ease your minds and prove to you that my motivations and methods are beyond reproach. Charles here has inspected my camera, and I have never touched *any* of the photographic plates I am about to use. Isn't that right, Charles?"

The crowd murmurs and Charles steps forward, holding the plates in his hand.

"Hand them here."

Charles doesn't give them to Mr. Spencer.

"Just one more thing, sir, if you don't mind," Charles says. He moves away, steps into the corner, and pulls out a case. Inside is the exact same model of camera that Mr. Spencer uses.

"In our early letters with Mr. Spencer, we asked what type of camera he used and purchased the same one in order to test his story. Please, sir, use *this* camera instead of your own."

"Well, look at you," Mr. Spencer spits, and I can see the cracks appearing in his mask and the real man oozing out. "So wise!"

He takes Charles's camera and handles it roughly, removing his from the tripod and setting it on the floor. He turns back to the crowd.

"I know what some of you must think. This is a hoax. Other spirit photographers have been exposed and that must mean we're *all* liars. Should I be judged by the worst in my field? I ask a modest sum for my work in order to support myself, not to get rich, and then people like this man here act as if—"

"You said yourself that the spirits are drawn to *you*, so the tools shouldn't matter," Charles interjects. And it is of no matter. Charles's prodding shouldn't get to him because he knows the plates are already changed by me, but I can see the anger bubbling in Mr. Spencer's eyes and hear it thick in his throat. Maybe his pride is hurt. Maybe he's pretending. It's hard to tell.

"You're an ugly presence to have in this room," he sneers. "I wouldn't be surprised if you scare the spirits away."

"Already planning your excuses, I see."

"They are *not* excuses, sir, they are the truth. A negative presence can repel the pure spirits away, and if you are to stay in this room you must—"

"In this house, I will stay wherever I wish," Charles says calmly and folds his arms. He's clearly used to being asked to leave, and comfortable with not obeying.

"Please sit," Mr. Spencer says, motioning at a man near the black curtain. He places his hat by the stool and the man drops money inside. "I apologize for the spectacle. No matter how hard I work, there will always be doubt. Who are you looking to connect with, sir?"

"My wife," the man says. "She died last May, but I still . . . I don't know . . . sometimes I think . . ."

"Do you feel her here now?"

The man nods, and Mr. Spencer closes his eyes and breathes in deeply.

"I feel her, too."

Mr. Spencer rubs his fingers over the plates and pulls one with a single drip of candle wax out from the stack and slides it into Charles's camera.

"Sit still. Don't move. Keep your eyes open and look here," he says, motioning to the lens.

There's a stillness in the basement—no one moves, no one breathes. The shutter clicks, the flash ignites, and the photographic plate gathers the light through the lens.

From the corner of the room, John motions at me to join him, and I slide my back along the wall, careful that no one sees me.

We retreat into a shadowy corner, and I stare at my shoes, trying not to look at him in case Charles notices us together.

"Did you find the plates?"

"Of course," I whisper. "But it wasn't easy."

"There are so many people here. It's going to be a lot of work."

"I know. I wish I had your help."

Charles turns and nods at me and my heart races in my chest. Did he see me talking to John? Does it matter? We're the only two kids here. Of course we would talk to each other. That's normal, isn't it?

Still, I walk away, trying to look innocent, but I know that the more I try, the more guilty I look.

Don't ruin it, Liza.

"Next," Mr. Spencer says, sliding out the plate and storing it in darkness. A woman places crumpled dollars in the hat, sits on the stool, and talks with Mr. Spencer. On and on it goes, the stories of loss and sadness blending together. As the supplies dwindle down, he's careful to select his subjects based on my wax markings. When the plates are all used, Charles springs into action, grabbing them and unscrewing the camera from the tripod.

"Ladies and gentlemen, I thank you all for your participation," Charles says. He pats the package of plates. "I will handle the development of the photos and the truth will soon be revealed. If this proves to be a fraud, we will return your money."

Mr. Spencer retreats to the corner of the room and takes a small bottle from his jacket, unscrews it, and takes a long sip. He smirks at Charles and eyes up the bills from his hat.

"Now, follow me to the assembly hall," Charles says. "Ms. Eldridge and Annabelle are waiting for us."

He tucks the package of photographic plates into his jacket and waves me over.

"We'll develop these after the assembly and find out once and for all what that man truly is," he says with a look confident that he would find no ghosts in Mr. Spencer's photos.

ANNABELLE

Charles leads the group of guests into the yard, where Ms. Eldridge is standing at the stone wall. Her arms are raised, and the sun is beating down on her face. The air is crisp, and I wrap my arms around my body to keep warm.

"Is he finished with his pictures?" she asks Charles, sensing that he's behind her without looking.

"He is."

"And?"

"I don't know. I couldn't spot any tricks."

"I see."

She spins to face the crowd, smiles, and says, "Good morning. Annabelle is eager to talk to us today. Shall we?"

The group follows her to the assembly hall. Mr. Spencer joins them, and John stays close beside him. Fox weaves throughout the people, her ears pointed up and her tail wagging. She yips at John and he pets her head. The little dog seems to have lived her life around crowds, knows how to blend in and be loved.

We arrive at the assembly hall and Ms. Eldridge unlocks its blue door and pets Fox's head.

"Wait here, girl," she says, then looks at me. "Dogs are very sensitive to spirits."

I follow her inside. The assembly hall is separate from the main house and not nearly as nice. It looks like it was cobbled together with spare parts. The paint is chipped, the beams warped, and the windows are cracked and covered with boards that only let in thin slivers of light. There's a makeshift stage built from old wood in the front, lit with a row of candles. A white curtain hangs behind it, and metal stars and ribbons are tied to the rafters, just like in that strange spot I found in the woods. Benches line the room, neatly arranged, but facing the back.

There's an uneasy silence in the air. I sit in the corner, as far away from the door as possible, and Charles comes beside me.

"Don't be scared," he whispers.

Soon, the room is filled and the benches are packed with people.

Margaret walks around the room and stares into each person's face, holding her hands up, like she's sensing things beneath the skin that only she can feel.

"You," she says, and points to a woman in the second row from the back. "Stand."

The woman is old and clutches a scarf against her chest. "Me?" she says, but there's something strong and clear in her voice that doesn't match her body.

Ms. Eldridge waves her hands over her, staying a few inches from touching her dress.

"Yes. Her energy is wrong. Charles, lead this woman out," Ms. Eldridge commands. "She isn't here with honest intentions. She is *not* one of us."

The woman shuffles out of the aisle, and Charles holds her elbow and helps her out the door.

"You're working with the devil!" she yells from outside, and Mr. Spencer smiles at me.

"A nonbeliever," Ms. Eldridge explains. "We cannot have this in Annabelle's presence."

It dawns on me why he was smiling. Just like Mr. Spencer has a routine before he takes a photograph to establish trust, that old woman was probably paid to sit here and be ushered out. This must be part of their lie, because if Ms. Eldridge and Margaret could really tell a person's true intentions just by looking at them, she'd have thrown Mr. Spencer out at first glance and I'd be left on the road to freeze.

Margaret makes her way through the rest of the rows, and when she's done, she stands near the stage. Ms. Eldridge takes the stairs beside the stage and stands in front of the curtain. It's clear she is the only one allowed to be there. I twist my head and watch as she hangs a small bell on a stick and clutches her hands as if she's praying.

"Only those with open minds to the spirit world should be in the presence of Silver Star," Ms. Eldridge says. Her eyes are closed, and her face is pointed to the ceiling. "If any among you doubt what is about to happen, please leave."

No one moves.

Margaret walks down the aisle and kneels beside me. She whispers in my ear, close enough to make the hair stand up on my neck, "Don't peek, darling. Look ahead and never turn back."

John looks at me and tilts his head.

Ms. Eldridge begins, her booming voice filling the room.

"Annabelle, we are here, prepared for your presence. Come to us. Connect us with your guiding light."

John taps his foot, and it's the only sound I can hear in the room, a beating in my ears.

Tap tap tap.

"Annabelle, we are waiting."

Silence, except the sound from John's shoes on the floor.

Tap tap tap.

I stare at him, try to a send a message with my eyes. *Stop it!*

"Annabelle," Ms. Eldridge says again, so quiet that I can hardly hear. The bell begins to ring, slowly at first and then faster and faster until it's one long note. They must be shaking the stick somehow. I want to look back and see, to discover their tricks. I force myself not to.

The wind blows outside and comes in through the cracks around the windows, extinguishing the row of candles and filling the room with the smell of smoke.

I squint to look through the little cracks around the window. Outside, the limbs of the oak tree are blowing and slivers of light come in the room. Dark gray clouds fill the sky. Inside, shadows dance around, circling me. They look almost human in the way they move. Does the shadow belong to Ms. Eldridge, or someone else?

They move quickly, and their forms are fleeting, but I swear I see eyes like two circles of white. No—it was just the specks of sunlight I saw through the window, leaving spots in my vision. I feel light-headed. The room seems to spin around me, and my arms go numb.

I glance over to John, see him look at me, wide-eyed. He covers his face with his hands.

Ms. Eldridge lets out a moan and then a voice says, "I am here." The voice sounds nothing like her own. It's caramel smooth and distant, somehow echoing against the walls of the assembly hall.

"Annabelle," Margaret says, "thank you for joining us."

"What do you ask of me?" the voice replies, and a light comes from the stage, bright yellow like the sun, glowing on the back of the crowd's heads.

Where is it coming from? How are they doing this? I don't dare look back, afraid I might melt into a pillar of salt like that poor lady in the Bible.

More shadows surround me, darker now, and if I squint I can see shoulders and heads and—

"Annabelle, we are here as true believers, wishing to speak through you." Margaret's voice is firm and controlled, like she's practiced this many times.

"Very well," the voice says.

I close my eyes, feel my heart beat in my chest, fill my ears with a pounding rush of blood. I can hardly breathe.

Margaret moves through the room, holding her hands over each person.

"You," she says to a woman. "Stand."

The woman obeys, and the voice coming from Ms. Eldridge says, "Your name is Elizabeth. Your child was lost to disease, but he has come to talk to you."

The light brightens and dims with her every word.

"He asks if you remember swimming in the pond?"

"Yes," the woman says. Her voice trembles. "I remember."

"He wants you to know there's a pond where he is, and it's beautiful. He can swim every day."

The woman cries out, clapping her hands, and I want to scream at them to stop.

This isn't right. Somehow, these lies feel worse than what we do with the pictures.

The woman continues asking questions to Annabelle, her eyes full of tears, until finally she sits back down beside her husband and he wraps an arm around her.

Margaret moves on, holding her hands over people. She stops over a man who lost his son in the war, another man who lost his wife to the flu, a woman whose husband was in an accident. The voice speaks to each of them. She knows their names and tells them things I probably could have guessed just by looking at them.

Everyone's story is basically the same, Mr. Spencer once told me. *Just a few little changes here and there.*

Margaret works her way down the aisle. Her hands pass over Mr. Spencer and move toward John.

"Stop," the voice commands.

Margaret looks back, surprised. Normally, it must be her that picks the people, but this time the voice has chosen.

"Him."

"Me?" Mr. Spencer asks, sitting up straight. He's smiling, eyes closed, basking in the silliness of their act.

"No. The boy," the voice says.

People murmur, and suddenly Mr. Spencer's face turns grim. He looks around, locking eyes with me.

What did you tell them? his face seems to say.

The light from the stage is brighter now, and the shadows are a deep, dark black, moving around the room, unmistakable. Can't other people see them, too?

"Stand," the voice commands, and I watch my brother grab the bench in front of him and push up from his seat. His legs are weak, and he coughs into his hand. He looks so frail all hunched over, but in my mind I see him as he was before the sickness came, running through fields of bright, tall grass, his fingers brushing a row of Mother's flowers, pulling a purple one for me to tuck into my hair. I chased him then, scooping him into my arms and crashing to the ground. We rolled in the sunlight, laughing, unaware of how our lives could change so quickly.

"You've suffered so much loss," the voice says.

He doesn't answer, but I don't think it was a question.

My hands tighten into fists. I want to stand and yell.

"It is your time now," the voice says. "Come to me. I need to show you something."

Mr. Spencer stomps his foot.

"Stop this!" he yells. Is this another test? A way to catch Mr. Spencer in his lies?

"Bring the boy to me," the voice commands, and I hear a ringing in my ears and the shadows tighten around me as the light from the stage pulses, getting brighter and brighter. Sparks move about, like white eyes staring through me.

John turns toward the stage, and I can't help myself any longer. I glance back and see Margaret frozen between the stage and John's bench. This doesn't seem to be part of their normal routine, but she moves toward John. When she's close, Mr. Spencer grabs her by the wrist.

"Whatever you women think you're doing here, I want you to *stop it*."

"Let go of me, you snake!" Margaret yells, slapping him across the face. This is the moment Charles was waiting for. He moves in and wraps his arm around Mr. Spencer's chest. He pulls him out the door, sending a burst of daylight into the dark assembly hall. For a moment the shadows seem to disappear.

Outside, I can hear Mr. Spencer yelling at Charles, and guests whisper to each other and try to listen.

"Bring the boy to me!" the voice yells, louder this time, terrifying.

John looks at me and I shake my head.

I turn my head and stare right into the streak of light on the stage. It seems to hover in the air behind Ms. Eldridge. Shadows snake around it and shapes move inside it, but they're so bright I can't see them clearly.

The light focuses on my face. I clench my fists, feeling as if my fingers have turned to salt. I want to turn away, but I can't. Colors pulse in the brightness and spots appear around me. A woman moves like she is in water, floating in the bright rays of light, her arms outstretched.

Is someone hiding behind the curtain? I look for signs of the trick. Heat radiates from the fabric.

What's happening?

Margaret comes beside me and grabs my face, steps between me and the light.

"I told you not to look," she whispers. I stare into her eyes and I feel like I'm drowning in her face. The chair feels alive beneath me. The corners of my vision darken, and I feel myself swaying.

I can't see.

A gentle rain starts to fall, pittering against the windows, and the shadows wrap around me, devouring me, and it's just like falling asleep. My body relaxes. It feels like the shadows are grabbing me, pulling me with them, into the darkness and back through the light.

It's a dream. I'm surrounded by greens and blues and golds. The sunlight on a summer day. My skin burns and the ringing sound continues in my ears, building until it's all I can hear.

And then . . . *nothing*.

When I open my eyes, I'm on the floor and two shapes are above me. The rain has stopped, and the door to the assembly hall is open, letting in a shaft of light.

Charles leans in, asks, "Is she all right?"

Margaret smiles and rubs my cheek.

"I think she will be."

"What did you see?" Ms. Eldridge asks, speaking with her own voice now. I don't know how long I was out, but the guests have gone into the yard. John's there, too, waiting for me. Mr. Spencer is nowhere to be seen, though I can hear him cursing at others to leave him alone.

"Nothing," I whisper. "I didn't see anything."

"Charles, get the girl some water," Ms. Eldridge says, returning to the stage.

She leans her large body on the pulpit, trembling slightly. She's shaken, and if that's fake as well, she's good at acting.

Charles helps me to my feet and holds my hand, guiding me to the door.

"What should I do with Mr. Spencer?" Charles asks, and now I remember what just happened between him and Charles, what that voice said to John, and the fear shoots through me. Have I ruined things already?

"Develop his pictures," Ms. Eldridge says. "I believe I know what you'll find."

I doubt that.

Charles nods, and when I'm finally able to stand, I follow him out of the chapel, back into the sunlight, hoping my work is good enough to save us.

DEVELOPING

Outside, guests surround Mr. Spencer, blocking him from the assembly hall. He tries to push through them to get to Charles, but they shove him back.

"Leave him for now," Charles says. "His time is coming."

Mr. Spencer smugly spits on the ground and brushes off his suit jacket. I can see that he's still angry, but he smiles and limps over to the porch and sits on a rocking chair, winking at me as I follow Charles into the house and into the dining room.

There's a pitcher of lukewarm water on a cart, and he pours me a tall glass. I down the whole thing without stopping, and soon I'm feeling completely fine, like whatever had happened in the assembly hall was a faraway dream. I was just tired. That's all.

"I'm sorry if we scared you," Charles says to me. "Are you all right?"

I nod.

"What happened?" he asks, staring into my eyes.

"The light was so bright," I say. "And then . . . did you see them too? The shadows?"

He doesn't answer. He seems to be searching for the right words, but unable to find them.

"Is it always like that?"

"Every time with Annabelle is different."

"How did they do it?"

"I'm not sure what you mean," he says, staring out the window and into the yard, deep in thought. Then he adjusts his glasses and taps his knuckles on the package of plates. "Come. Let's discover the truth about our friend Mr. Spencer."

We walk through the house until we arrive at a small door under a staircase. Charles unlocks it, revealing a tight, windowless room that smells of chemicals. The ceiling is slanted at such a harsh angle that I have to kneel in the corner, tucking my knees to my chest. I like being in the dark. It's where I'm most comfortable.

Charles pulls a cord that lights a red bulb, casting the room in a bloody glow. He sets the photographic plates on the table, then organizes jars and pans.

"What do you think we'll find on these?" he asks.

"I don't know," I whisper.

"*Nothing* is my guess, and then we can put this all behind us."

Charles pours chemicals into the first pan and

dips the photographic plate into it.

"What I was trying to tell you earlier was that it's normal to have doubt, Liza. I often do, too. Perhaps I shouldn't admit that. Maybe I am a negative presence in this place, though I try my best not to be. Faith comes easier for other people. Margaret is a true believer."

He smiles when he says her name, and I think of her picture in his room.

"Still, I can't deny how I feel here, like we really are at a thin place between worlds."

"Yes," I say, thinking back to the chill that shot down my arms when I came through the gate.

"I've never thought much of spirit photography, to be honest. There are too many ways to trick someone. If spirits can't be seen by the eye, how can they be seen by a lens?"

He continues to work, and I watch as the chemicals mix. Mr. Spencer never let me watch him develop pictures before. He acted like it was some great secret that only he could know, probably afraid that I'd take John and run away to start up our own business. And maybe he's right. I study Charles, watching him move with an ease that's almost hypnotic.

He notices me staring and says, "Come closer, I'll show you how this works."

He explains what each chemical does, how it interacts

with the coating on the glass and forms the negative image, a reverse of reality, where the dark is light and the light is dark.

I watch as the faint shapes begin to form, hoping the ghosts I created are good enough to fool him.

He breathes out in a sharp burst as the image comes into focus.

"Impossible," he says, stopping to inspect the plate he's developing and waves at me to look.

In the negative, I can make out the faint shadow of a woman surrounding a man. Her cotton dress looks black in the reverse, swirling around his shoulders, and her eyes are so bright.

He rinses the plate, moves it to the stop bath, and covers the tray with a towel, then kicks open the door and runs down the hall. I'm not sure if I should follow, but I do anyway. I have to know if he believes what he saw.

"Ms. Eldridge!" he calls out, and when there is no reply, he turns and walks through the kitchen where three cooks are preparing lunch.

"Have you seen Ms. Eldridge?"

"She's out back, sir. By the tree," one of them says, and Charles opens a side door and runs through the grass. I walk behind at a steady pace, keeping my face as blank as possible.

John is standing beside Margaret in the front yard,

studying the house. He looks at me as I walk past and I raise my eyebrows. He nods.

"What's wrong, Charles?" Margaret asks.

"Follow me," he says, and takes her hand and pulls her through the yard, toward the large oak tree that towers over the wall where Ms. Eldridge is standing.

"I exchanged his camera with my own, ma'am. I bought new plates and kept them in my room. I watched his every move, developed the photographs myself, and—"

Ms. Eldridge doesn't turn.

"What's wrong?" he asks.

"She's still very weak from this morning," Margaret says. "The thin place has never been open that wide before, and—"

But Charles is barely listening, waving away her words. "There's no other way he could have done it. I think Mr. Spencer actually has a gift."

There's silence at that, but finally Ms. Eldridge speaks. Her voice sounds small and fragile.

"Do you really believe that?"

"I do."

Relief floods through me. We can stay longer. John can sleep in his warm bed and he'll get better. Word will get around that we're telling the truth, and money will keep coming in. Everything will be fine now.

"And what do you think, little one?"

It takes me a moment to realize she's talking to me. Once again, she knows who is here without looking. How does she do it? Is it a guess, or some sort of trick?

"It was . . . I thought . . ." The words don't come easily. No one has ever asked what I thought. "It looked real to me."

"Very good. Charles, finish developing his pictures. I suspect we'll need more supplies once word gets out, but return the money to the guests from our own coffers. For the time being, I'll pay for it all. Margaret, find out if there's anything Mr. Spencer needs. We'll keep him comfortable."

"You don't have to do this," Margaret says. "We can make him leave."

"I must. This is my mission."

Ms. Eldridge holds out her hand and touches the stone wall.

Margaret looks like she has more she wants to say but decides against it. She walks toward the house, past John, slipping inside.

Ms. Eldridge turns to look at me.

"How do you feel?"

Her eyes seem to pierce through me, and I stare at my shoes and mutter, "Fine."

"I can tell you are a girl with strong powers. I

sensed it the moment you entered this place. You must be careful here and listen to our instructions."

"Yes, ma'am," I say, hoping this ends the conversation.

She whispers something to Charles and he leads me back to the house, through a thin, twisting hallway that comes out, as if by magic, near the little door of the darkroom.

We work on developing the rest of the plates all through the morning and long past lunch.

"Have you ever seen anything so astonishing?" Charles asks, eyeing the faint shape of a ghost on another plate. My stomach rumbles, but Charles doesn't hear it. He's absorbed in the work, going through the stack and then using a tool called an enlarger to shine a light through the plate onto a piece of special paper. After that, the image appears like magic when put in the developing fluid. It amazes me every time, watching people appear from nothing onto the paper. When he's finished, he clips the photos to a thin string that hangs along the top of the room to dry.

"Would you like to be my assistant?" Charles asks. "You can guard the supplies from Mr. Spencer and help me develop the photographs. I'll teach you how all this works. What do you say?"

I want to scream out, hug him, jump up and down.

I can't believe my good luck.

"I'd like that," I say, hoping he doesn't notice just how excited I am. "I'd like that very much."

By the time he's done developing all of the plates, it's early evening, and he leads us out near the front of the house. We go on the porch, where people are sitting on wooden chairs and drinking tea. There's a prayer circle on the grass and a group standing around the tree, singing hymns. The dark clouds and wind have gone away, and their off-key notes seem to float up into the deep blue sky.

Charles and I walk past rows of black automobiles parked beside the stone wall and up to a carriage hitched beside the gate. He sits inside and waves at me to join him.

"We need to go into town to get more supplies for Mr. Spencer," he says, whipping the reins. The horse lurches forward and pulls us through the gate and up the road, turning at a fork in the road with deep grooves from other wheels. "To be honest, this is a trip I didn't expect to make."

The carriage bounces toward town, down roads flanked by trees. Fallen leaves crunch under our wheels, and birds call out to us.

Charles turns to me.

"The town's a few miles away, so we have some time," he says. "Why don't you tell me your story?

There must be an interesting tale as to how a young girl ended up cold and near death by the side of the road."

I shrug. Any lie I tell him will be one more thing to remember, so the less I say, the better.

"I could ask around in town. Maybe there's someone looking for you."

"There's no one," I say, and he smiles at me, his mustache curling at the corners like a caterpillar.

"Then who are you running from?" he asks, and I look at my toes, remembering the last place we stayed—Rochester, New York—and the reason we had to leave so fast.

We lived in a row home deep in the city, where men walked the streets telling stories of the war, and the fear of the flu was still around us. I hated it there. It was hot and dusty, and our house smelled sour. John and I stayed in the back room, hidden from the guests, listening to clients tell Mr. Spencer their sad stories. Boxes of photographic plates piled up on every surface of the room, and there was so much work to do.

Every day it was the same. Cut, cut, cut, glue, glue, glue, click, click, click.

My back hurt from hunching over the camera, and my fingers refused to move.

"We need to get you outside," I told John that

night, and he shook his head.

"We can't."

"You need fresh air. You'll never get better in here."

He coughed into his fist and his thin body trembled.

"See?"

"All right," he said. "Just for a little bit."

When Mr. Spencer had settled in and all was silent, I cracked open the window and pulled John out into the alley behind the house.

"Walk with me," I said, and helped him down the alley, breathing in the night air. We went out the gate to the sidewalk and watched people in automobiles pass by us, unaware of the strange ghost children waiting in the shadows.

"It's beautiful here," John said.

"No. It's ugly and gray. I wish we could go back home."

I put my arm around him. We took in the smells of the street and studied the rows of narrow buildings lit by the orange glows of the streetlights.

I heard something moving in the alley behind us and saw a man in the darkness. He cupped his hands and peered into our window.

Good, he didn't see we were outside. I pulled John close, hiding behind the gate.

"We shouldn't have come out here," John said.

"Quiet," I whispered.

"He knows we're here," John said, a bit too loud.

The man stood frozen, looking in our direction, and I pulled John closer, tucking our bodies close to the wall of the alley, trying to blend in with the bricks.

"Hello," the man whispered. "You there. Come here."

The man walked toward us. He stepped into the glow of the moon, and I could see he was pencil thin and wore a blue suit and bowler hat. He looked familiar. I had seen him through the crack in our door earlier that week. He had come to us and told Mr. Spencer a story about his daughter, but something wasn't right. Mr. Spencer must have sensed it, too, because he refused to take his picture. Detectives have a way about them, trying too hard to blend in, asking too many questions. Easy to spot if you're looking.

"Did you come from this house?" the man asked, pointing.

I didn't answer, and I squeezed John's arm so he wouldn't, either.

"Are you with Mr. Spencer?" he asked, stepping closer. "I just have some questions. Don't be scared."

"Follow me," I whispered, so quiet that I wasn't sure if any sound left my lips.

"I know Spencer's a liar," the man said. "I just need to find his secret. We'll take care of you."

Wrapping my arm around John's chest, I lifted him to his feet and pulled him onto the sidewalk. I ran across the road, hardly even letting John's feet touch the ground, turning the corner and ducking into the first alley I found.

"Stop!" the man called out, but we were too fast.

We nestled into a pile of trash and held our breaths as the man's shoes clicked on the sidewalk.

"I'm not going to hurt you," he called out. I stayed with John, our bodies wrapped together in the shadows, waiting a long time until the street was quiet and I was certain he was gone.

"Let's go."

"I'm not sure I can run."

"I'll help you."

I looped my arm around him, and we raced back to the alley behind our house and crawled back through the window.

I told Mr. Spencer everything. I had to. He was mad, of course, but the heat was on and the water was bubbling. Soon it would be boiling. If we didn't leave soon, it would burn us all.

The detective's voice echoed in my head. *I just have some questions.*

What did he want to ask me?

"You ruin everything," Mr. Spencer hissed that night.

"Liza?" Charles asks, and suddenly I'm back in the carriage, out of my thoughts. "You don't have to tell me what you're running from. But I'd understand."

"No," I say. "You wouldn't."

GLENSBORO

Our carriage turns down a road surrounded by trees and rolling fields. We crest the hill and see a small town below, hardly more than a cluster of buildings separated by a crisscross of streets. There's a short row of homes along the outskirts, slowly blending into sloping fields and a wide river to the left.

"Here we are," Charles says. "Glensboro."

The road turns from dirt to cobblestone, and Charles steers the carriage around the back roads and hitches the horse to a post beside an alley.

"We're going in the back," Charles says, pointing at a chipped wooden door. "Mr. Muller is a nice man, but he doesn't like others to see me in his store. He thinks it will scare away business."

He says *nice* in a way that makes me think Mr. Muller isn't nice at all.

The door is unlocked but Charles still taps twice before entering.

"Come in!" a voice calls, and Charles enters, waving at me to follow.

"Ah, Charles!" Mr. Muller says from behind the counter. "Didn't expect to see you today, my boy."

Mr. Muller is barrel-chested, with a gray vest and a white shirt rolled up to his forearms. Thin, wire spectacles balance on the edge of his round nose, and he coughs and wipes his mouth with a handkerchief.

"Don't worry, it's just allergies. I'm as healthy as can be."

He looks at me and nods disapprovingly.

"Who's the girl?" Mr. Muller asks, eyeing me suspiciously, like he doesn't trust Charles to be responsible for me.

"A visitor to the Society. She's helping me with the photos."

"Of course she is! She looks like a guest to the *Loony* Star, doesn't she?"

Charles smiles at him.

"So, what can I do for you?"

"I need more photographic plates. Same as the last time, sir, if you have them."

"So soon?" Mr. Muller says. He goes into a small room behind the counter and slides a step stool beside a shelf. "Let me see. Dry plate. Four by five inches?"

"Yes, sir."

Mr. Muller removes a box from a top shelf and flips through it, removing a large package.

"This is all I have. I'm going into Philadelphia early next week and could get more if you'd like."

"That would be wonderful, thank you. I'll take all you have for now."

"You should switch to film, Charles, it's much cheaper."

"So I've heard."

"How many plates should I get for you?"

"As many as you can. One hundred, at least. I suspect we'll be needing them, and perhaps more after word gets out."

One hundred. My fingers already ache at the thought of the work ahead of me.

"Very good," Mr. Muller says. "Though I *will* need a sizable down payment in order to—"

Charles places a neat fold of bills on the counter and tucks the packages under his arm. He nods and points me back to the door.

"That girl, did her parents let her come with you?"

"They didn't say otherwise," Charles answers calmly.

It's true, I suppose.

"What's your name, little darling?" Mr. Muller

asks, but I don't answer. I don't like him.

"She's a shy one," Charles explains, turning to wink at me.

Mr. Muller stares at me, like he's trying to decide if he should press the issue further, but finally he slaps his hands on the counter and says, "Good doing business with you."

Charles smiles and nods at him. "Have a good evening, sir."

Back in the carriage, he takes the reins and passes the package of plates to me.

"Here you are," he says. "Make sure no one touches them, especially Mr. Spencer."

I squeeze the box and smile. No more sneaking through the house, no more stealing plates and staying up all night to work. It's almost too easy.

The carriage pulls us out of town and over hills, back through the trees and toward the Society. It's silent, but the pleasant sort. Calm. The air is cool, and the sounds of the horses and the rhythm of the wheels comfort me. The sun has almost set, giving the sky a light-purple tint. I lean against the side of the carriage and wish I could sleep.

"We've missed dinner," Charles says, glancing at his pocket watch. "Here's hoping they saved us something."

The horses turn the corner, passing a tall clump of trees, and we can see the Silver Star Society at the bottom of the valley.

More guests are outside now, singing and dancing, and their cries echo up the hill. There's a row of lanterns resting on the wall, lighting the yard.

We hitch the carriage and go inside. There are two plates of food waiting for us on the dining room table, and we eat together, enjoying the silence between us. Charles finishes first and goes upstairs to his room, and John appears in the doorway. Fox ambles beside him and leans her head against his leg.

"Where were you?" he asks. I've never left him this long without telling him, and I feel guilty that I didn't look for him first.

"Not here," I say, trying not to move my mouth.

I doubt Charles can hear us from upstairs, but the large front window overlooks the darkness of the yard, and the light over the table makes me feel like we're onstage. I can't see out, but everyone can see in.

"I was in town with Charles."

"Why? What's that?" he asks, eyeing the package beside me.

I motion him to move into the corner of the room, out of view of the window, and whisper, "We were getting supplies. You won't believe it. Charles asked me to *guard them* from Mr. Spencer."

His eyes narrow. Not the reaction I expected.

"I don't like it here," he says.

"I don't, either," I say, but that's not completely true. Charles has been kind to me, and the bed is soft and warm. The shadows I've seen are only in my mind, I'm sure of that now.

"We need to leave," he says, and I want to stand up and hug him but know that I can't. I stare at my plate, move the food around with my fork.

"Is it because of Annabelle's voice and the light?" I ask. "You know that's all fake. Just like our photos."

He seems to think on this as he rubs the spot behind Fox's ear.

"What did you see in the assembly hall?" he asks, and I think back to the ball of light and the strange shapes that surrounded the room.

"Nothing. I don't know. I was just tired."

"Is that why you fainted?"

Now I can see in his eyes that it's not just the voice that's worried him, it was also me. I should have told him I was fine, but I was in the darkroom developing, and then in Glensboro. I never considered how he must have felt.

"Really, John, nothing's wrong. And as for what happened in the assembly hall, I'll show you there's nothing to be worried about."

"How?"

"Tonight. Once everyone is asleep, meet me outside. We'll see for ourselves."

Their lie may be big, but that doesn't mean there isn't a simple explanation.

Is it him I want to convince or myself?

There's a sound in the front hallway and Ms. Eldridge walks down the hall, coming from the room with Madam Crimson's cabinets. She was moving quietly. I didn't know she was inside, and hope that she didn't hear our whispers.

Her hair is unclipped and wild, and she looks much different than last night, when everything about her seemed perfectly in place. I stare at my plate, pretending I don't see John. He tucks his body deeper into the corner of the room.

She smiles at me from the doorway and eyes my plate.

"Are you finished?"

"Yes, ma'am," I say, hardly able to breathe.

Please don't come in. Please don't see him with me.

"I'm sorry to do this, but we have more people arriving tonight and we'll need your room."

Outside, I hear the roar of a motor over the singing. More people have arrived, and guests are calling out greetings, welcoming them into the Society.

Ms. Eldridge motions at me to stand and leads me upstairs. When we get to my room, she picks up my suitcase, grunting at the surprising weight of it. I hear the camera slide along the bottom, hit the side, and I pray she doesn't open it.

"I can carry that," I say, but she ignores me. She opens the hall closet and removes a stack of thick wool blankets.

"You'll carry these, dear. We'll put you downstairs, and you'll need them to keep warm."

We walk down a tight, looping staircase in the back of the house and she opens another door that leads down more steps.

I realize now what she means. *Downstairs* doesn't mean the first floor—it means the basement.

We go deeper down and arrive at a small door that opens to the opposite end of the large center room where Mr. Spencer took photographs this morning. His backdrop and tripod are still up, but it feels different at night. Haunted, somehow, and from down here the singing outside sounds like animals howling.

She leads me to the rear corner of the basement, where there's a little storage room with a cot and a table inside. There's a window in the middle of the stone wall, which means this side isn't underground, and I'm thankful for that. Cold air seeps from the cracks around the frame.

"Please let me know if you need anything else,"

she says, and then hurries off before I can answer, leaving me alone with my things.

I sit on the bed, wrap the blankets around my shoulders, and feel the weight of the camera plates in my hand. It will be hours until the guests are in and John and I can explore the assembly hall. I could get started on the plates now, be finished in a few hours, and sleep, but what if someone saw me? What if one of the guests noticed the strange glow of my lantern from the window?

No.

It's better to be safe, at least for now.

I lie down, trying to clear my mind. Time passes, and I listen to the odd sounds that echo from upstairs down to the basement—shutters clank and boards moan. The doors to the outhouses open and close.

Then I hear a loud thumping sound. I look out of my room and see motion in the corner of the basement. Dark shadows move about, but it's too dim to see anything. Is it the same shadows I saw earlier?

"John? Is that you?" I say out loud, but of course it isn't him. He couldn't get down those narrow stairs by himself. His legs are too weak, and besides—

Thump. Thump.

There it is again. A chill races down my arms, and a voice in my head screams at me to run. I think I see a figure moving around the main room of the basement. It's one of the shadows, isn't it? I slip out of the room, swiftly making my way to the door that leads outside, when a hand grabs my shoulder.

I can smell Mr. Spencer's breath before I turn to see him. His grip is hard, but he sways with the wind. I could knock him over if I wanted to.

"Let go!" I hiss.

"Cozying up real nice to Charles, aren't you?" he whispers, holding tight.

"I'm not *cozying* up to anyone," I say, trying to sound firm in my words. "He thinks I'm his friend. And he's going to let me guard the camera supplies, so you should be thanking me."

I point to my little corner room in the basement, where the package is waiting for me.

Mr. Spencer smiles broadly at this.

"Well, if that ain't the fox guarding the henhouse. What all have you told him?"

"Nothing. Just my name."

His grip tightens. "That's too much."

"Well, I can't stay completely silent forever. Talking to him is what got him to trust me, and if—"

He doesn't let me finish. He grabs my jaw, looking around the room to make sure we're alone.

"Have you talked to John around them?" he asks.

"No."

He can see the lie in my eyes.

"Just a bit this morning. And he was in the dining room with me tonight and—"

"Don't do this to us, Liza. Not *here.*"

"I didn't do anything," I whisper.

"You're a liar. What do they know about us?"

"Nothing. I promise."

He releases his grip and I fall back, rubbing my chin. I stare at his shoes and he continues to talk, whispering awful things to me, but my ears are buzzing with rage and I don't listen. He spits on the ground and turns, heading back to the stairs.

"Get to work, Liza," he says. "And watch yourself. This place isn't like the others. If we get caught here, there will be hell to pay."

I nod and slink back into my room. I shut the door and curl into my bed, wrapping the wool blankets around me. Out the window, all I see is blackness. The lanterns are off, and the guests are inside. The singing has stopped in the yard and I can hear footsteps above in the entry hall.

This place isn't like the others.

No, it certainly isn't. I've felt it since the moment I arrived, the strangeness of everything. Ms. Eldridge is different. She's smarter than other people I've met along the way. She's certainly smarter than Mr. Spencer, but it just makes me want to figure out her secrets even more.

I wait in my room for the right time to get John. Tonight, we'll search the assembly hall and find the truth.

But what is truth without proof? And just like that, another idea comes.

I grab the box of photographic plates and open my Hidden Place, working in the dark, removing a plate and placing it into the wooden holder, then sliding it into the back of my camera.

I'm tired of letting things happen to me. Events seem to crash over me like waves, spinning me in whatever direction the current flows. For once, I want to be in control.

One picture, that's all I need.

The thrill of the idea pounds in my head. If I can get proof of their lies, I can keep us safe.

When the only sounds are the night breezes, I sneak into the basement and find Mr. Spencer's flash and bottle of powder. Then I lift the beam to the back door and slip into the night, cradling the camera against my chest.

I circle the house, hoping John is still awake and watching for me. Soon, I see his small shape moving beside the wall, limping along, his breath rattling in his chest.

"Let's go," I say, and I stand behind him and lead him back to the assembly hall.

THE ASSEMBLY HALL

I hold the camera in one arm and loop the other around John's waist. Cold air blows down the valley, and the moon peeks out from the clouds, lighting the yard in little blobs of blue.

Darkness swells over the assembly hall like a drop of ink has been squirted into the sky. The small building is covered in shadows, a black square in the yard. I see a shadow move across the side of the house but I run past it, not looking at the shape. There's nothing there. Everything can be explained. I'll prove that tonight.

The assembly hall's door is locked, but the glass pane of the boarded-up window is loose, so I slide the camera under the window, then crawl inside the narrow gap. I pull John behind me. He kneels against the wall to steady himself.

"What are we looking for?" he asks.

"I don't know exactly," I say. "Her secret."

"But what if she doesn't have one?"

I smile and arch my eyebrow at him.

"How's a picture going to help us, anyway?"

"They can't kick us out if we have proof of what they're doing."

"Do you really want to stay here?"

"Just through the winter. Until you're feeling stronger."

The assembly hall seems smaller at night, and in the darkness, the metal stars look like bats hanging from the rafters.

"We shouldn't be here," John says.

My John. Always so careful. Always following the rules.

"It's all right," I say.

We walk around the room, and I rub my hands along the wall. This morning, the light from the cracks in the window and from behind the curtain on the stage painted the walls with gold. The shadows seemed alive around me, but at night the whole place seems gray and sleeping.

I examine every little detail. Why are the benches turned backward? Why did Margaret tell me not to look back? No one else was allowed on the stage, so something must be hidden there. I pace over to the small set of stairs, and they creak under my feet. I hang the little bell on the stick. It seemed to ring by itself this morning, like the spirits were touching it with their fingers. The wooden boards are old and soft around the stick, and I see now that if I push my toes on the floor beside it, the stick wiggles and the bell trembles and sounds, appearing as if it's moving on its own.

"Look at this," I say, ringing the bell faster with my foot. "It's a ghost!"

"Quiet, Liza."

Behind me hangs the white curtain. What was that strange light behind it? Was it really a glimpse into the other side, a door between the living and the spirits? Or was it only a magician's prop?

I walk up to take a closer look. The curtain is made of a thin material, and my hand wraps around the fabric and pulls it to the side, revealing—

Nothing.

I had hoped to see a giant light bulb, or a place for someone to hide, to speak as Annabelle, but the only thing behind the curtains are unpainted boards and a cracked window.

Maybe the sun was in the right position to shine through the window. Or maybe someone stood in the yard with a mirror, holding it at just the right angle to—

No. These ideas won't help me. I need solid proof of something, something that can't be denied.

"Liza?" John says, but I ignore him.

I keep searching, feeling frantic. If I can't find anything, does that mean—

"Liza," John says again. He stands at the window, looking out at the yard.

My fingers move along the boards of the stage, searching for anything out of place.

"Look!"

"What?"

"Someone's out there," John whispers.

"Mr. Spencer?"

John shakes his head and I grab the camera, run down the stage stairs, and hide it under a bench before joining him at the window.

A shadow moves in the yard, the same kind I saw last night in the reflection in the vase, the same thing I saw dancing around this room during the assembly. I thought I was tired, convinced myself it had all been in my mind, but if John sees them, too, then—

Suddenly, more shadows appear, rising from the ground, and wind howls through the window. The shadows move toward the assembly hall, staying in the darkness on the edges of the moonlight.

Rain begins to fall, and a crack of lightning rips through the sky.

The bolt hits the ground, and a ball of golden light seems to hover in the air. For a moment I think

I've gone blind, because it's so bright that it washes everything else away.

"John!" I call out.

I can't see him, but I can hear his voice beside me. "I'm here."

There's a buzzing in my ears, the same feeling I had this morning. I clutch my hands to my head and try not to faint again as more shadows pour from the light and slip through the windows, entering the assembly hall.

Shapes swarm around me, blobs in the brightness. It looks like daytime through the glow, and there are trees filling the valley. I can hear singing.

John speaks to me, and his voice seems a world away. The shape of a woman forms before me, but she's nearly too bright to look at.

She raises her arms and locks eyes with mine. Rays of light wrap around her, blurring her features.

"Annabelle?" I call out, but she doesn't answer.

The words Margaret told me ring in my ears: *We're at a thin place between the worlds of the living and the spirits.*

No. That's not possible.

That caramel-smooth voice comes from her lips, the sound wraps around.

"We have come to take him," she says. "You must let him go."

"No," I say. "I can't."

The woman frowns and seems to speak to the shadows now.

"Bring him to me now."

The light pulses, a hole torn through the night, and figures step through it and fill the yard.

The explosion has ripped the door to the assembly hall clean from its hinges, and the boards surrounding it are gone. Everything goes dark, and above me, I can hear the metal stars blow on their strings, clanging into each other. My eyes start to adjust.

Wind roars outside, and the heavy rain continues to fall. That dot of ink in the sky that was small when we first went into the assembly hall has spread out, overtaking the sky.

I spin, searching for John, trying to see him through the sparks of light blinking in my vision, and watch as the shadows move along the walls and break free. They surround him, their dark limbs twisting around his arms.

"John!" I scream, loud enough that I worry someone from the house might hear over the storm. I run to him, banging my knees against the benches, fighting to get to him.

The shadows pull him along the ground toward the door, and I wave my fists at them, grab for his ankles, trying to pull him back to me.

There's nothing I can do except hold on to him, but they're too strong. I swipe at them and my hands just pass through their bodies.

"Leave him!" I scream, and they stop for an instant and turn. In the darkness, I can see their faces. They're dim and grainy but certainly human, with sunken white eyes and dark lips, like the negative images on photographic plates. They move like sheets on a clothesline, blowing in the wind, and there's a certain shimmer around them.

John isn't fighting, but his eyes are wide, pleading for me to do something.

Think, Liza.

This morning, the shadows disappeared when Charles opened the door. Light is the opposite of shadows, every photographer knows that. But not any light will do—*light from this side.*

Even considering that makes me wonder if I've lost my mind.

I grab the flash and pour a little bit of powder into the trough. I hold the flash and aim the camera at the shadows, not even bothering to focus, and—

Click.

Boom.

The flash ignites and a burst of smoke hovers over my head. The room is filled with an angry light, a harsher type than the warm gold that was in the yard.

For an instant, I can see every corner of the hall, every ordinary bench and board. The shadowy figures burst apart into dark wisps and disappear before my eyes.

John lies in the aisle, breathing hard, his whole body trembling.

"Are you all right?" I ask, cradling his head in my arms.

"I think so. What happened?"

"I don't know," I say, not mentioning the other world I saw, and what the woman told me. It would only scare him.

They'll never take you, John. I promise.

I grab my camera and pull him out the hole where the door once was, lead him to the house.

As quickly as the dark clouds formed, they've disappeared. The rain has stopped, and the wind is faint.

I help John into the front door and then circle the house to the basement, slipping into my room. My heart is beating in my chest and I kneel in front of the door and press myself against it.

What were those things? And why do they want John?

I look out the window but the yard is empty now.

126

There's no way I can sleep tonight. I need to finish my work. When my breathing returns to normal, I open my suitcase and unhook the compartment to my Hidden Place, pulling out strands of cotton and a stack of newsprint faces that are ready to be cut.

I light the wick in my lantern, then get to work. I cut and glue, cut and glue, moving fast, trying to forget what I saw and to not consider what it means. It was nothing. Just a storm.

The lies we tell ourselves are the strongest kind.

When my ghost creations are ready, I prop them up by the wall and turn on the lantern until the light is bright enough to expose them. I place the box of photographic plates beside me.

I pull the plate I used in the assembly hall from the camera and wrap it in my sheet, then smash it against the ground, over and over, then dump the pieces into my Hidden Place.

More secrets to hide.

I press the camera's shutter, moving through the pictures.

Click.

Click.

Click.

Through my window, a silver star sparkles, alone in the black sky.

A FRAUD AMONG US

I finish half of the plates before the sun rises, and then mark them with candle wax and pack them inside, placing the tape that seals the box right where I found it.

I hear sounds on the basement steps, so I pack all of my things back into my Hidden Place and lie in bed, pulling the blanket up around my neck to hide my clothing. I shut my eyes, slow my breathing.

There's a light knock on the door and Charles opens it.

"Rise and shine," he says, opening the door to my room. The morning light comes through the little window and makes a square pattern on the floor.

"Did you guard these?" he asks, picking up the box of half-altered plates and rubbing his hands over the packaging.

"Yes."

Charles tucks the package under his arm and waits

outside the room. "Get dressed, we have much to do today."

I let a few minutes pass, enough to make him think I'm pulling on my clothes, and follow him upstairs. The house is bustling with people, and I have to press myself against the hallway wall to make it into the dining room.

Through the front window, I see a group of men examining the damage to the assembly hall. In the daylight, the hole looks bigger, a giant chunk ripped right from the front in a circular shape.

"A sudden storm must have passed through," a woman says. "Tore the planks right from the frame."

"We're lucky it didn't hit the house."

Many of the guests inside are the same as yesterday, but there are a few new faces, probably some locals here for a day, and others that look like they traveled a long distance.

I scan the room for Mr. Spencer, but don't see him among the others. John sits alone in a corner, silently watching people eat their breakfast, and Fox lies beside him.

Charles claps his hands in the center of the room to get everyone's attention.

"Excuse me, all. There will be no assembly with Silver Star this morning. We'll be working on repairing the damage."

A man with plump red cheeks stands and says, "That's the whole reason I came! Can't we do it somewhere else?" Other guests murmur in agreement.

"Very sorry for the inconvenience. Anyway, Ms. Eldridge is still feeling weak from yesterday. Perhaps it's for the best. Schedules for other events are posted around the grounds. There's still much to keep us busy. Ms. Van Heusen will be doing another painting demonstration in the front room, so please sign up if you're interested. Madam Crimson will be starting in the parlor in just a few moments for what I'm sure will be an interesting display, and later, Mr. Spencer will be taking photographs in the basement."

Charles sets the package of photographic plates beside me.

"You wait here," he says. "I'll get us some food."

I stay in the dining room, resting my hands on the photographic plates. The smells coming from the kitchen are amazing. I didn't think I was hungry, not after what I saw last night, but my stomach rumbles in betrayal.

Before Charles returns, Ms. Eldridge comes beside me and places a thick hand on my shoulder.

"There you are!" she says. "We'll be eating in the back room today."

Fox wags her tail beside John, and she points and says, "You can stay where you are."

Why did she say that to him? Did she see us talking?

"All right," John says, softly, and I can tell he's thinking the same thing.

Ms. Eldridge grabs my arm before I can pick up the box of photographic plates, leaving them unguarded on the table. Despite what Charles said, she doesn't look weak to me. She guides me through hallways, and we pass the front room where Ms. Van Heusen is setting up easels and brushes, preparing to create paintings while her hand is guided by spirits. The ones she has on display are bright, with looping white lines and eerie faces, creepy things that no one would want hanging in their house otherwise. We continue on, past the parlor where Madam Crimson sits, surrounded by her cabinet and trumpets. A crowd has gathered around her, including Mr. Spencer.

Finally, we arrive at a pantry beside the kitchen. Charles is standing, eating eggs from a plate, and nods at me.

"Sit down, dear. Eat," Ms. Eldridge says. I obey, taking small bites, even though it's odd to have them standing there, looking down their noses at me.

I don't know if they want me to talk first, so I sit quietly, moving the eggs around my plate.

"How are you liking your new room?" Ms. Eldridge says, breaking the silence.

"It's very nice."

"Did last night's storm wake you?"

"No, ma'am," I say. "Is that what happened to the assembly hall?"

She smiles.

"I suspect so. I hope it didn't frighten you. Do you know what causes the storms?"

I don't answer, afraid she's asking about the things I saw last night.

"There are things happening in the air that are invisible to our eyes, forces battling against each other. The heat from the ground rises, forms the clouds, collides with the coolness high up in the sky and creates an electrical charge. The positive charge and the negative charge fight against each other, sparking into a bolt of lightning that unleashes upon us."

I remember Mother telling John that to calm him when storms raged outside our window. Such a simple explanation for something so big and terrifying.

"Humans only recently learned these things. For centuries, storms were thought to be the work of the gods, or punishment for evil deeds. We are constantly learning, dear, replacing our superstitions for facts. Still, no one knows why a lightning bolt is shaped the way it is, or where it will strike."

She motions to Charles.

"Charles will fix the damage to the assembly hall, but I fear the storms have just begun. He told me you saw shadows yesterday."

I'm not sure if it's a question, but I nod, wishing I had kept my mouth shut.

"There are some things only children can see. Or perhaps it is simply that adult eyes cannot accept it. When I was a girl, I saw shadows too. When my grandmother died, I could still feel her presence around me. I wasn't able to let go of her. Annabelle was stuck between the worlds of the living and the dead, and when those worlds came too close, they crashed into each other, sparking like the particles in a cloud, forming lightning. The bolt scorched the trees around her gravestone, cut them clean in half, taking them out of this world and into hers. For a moment, if you can believe it, I felt like I was *there*, like the worlds had overlapped and I was in Summerland with the spirits. I stood with her in the trees, looked at the birds in the sky, felt the warm earth under my feet, and it was then that I realized I wasn't done with this side. I wanted to return. I wanted to *live* again."

Her story would be impossible for me to believe just a few days ago. But now that I've seen the light for myself, seen how it seemed to burst around us and eat up the wood surrounding the door to the assembly hall, I don't know what to think. But still, it's hard to believe when I know there are lies behind everything.

"Speaking to Annabelle has always been a risk, but one that we have managed so far. Things must remain in balance here. The thin place is all that separates us. Do you understand?"

"Yes, ma'am."

"I know you have a gift, and I want to help you if I can. But to do that, you need to be completely honest with me, and with yourself."

I nod, even though I don't mean it.

"Very well," she says, motioning at me to stand. "Follow me. You're about to see what we do to frauds here."

The ground feels like it's dropped from under me. Does she already know? Was this all a test or a way to get me to confess?

She leads us through the halls, back to the room with Mr. Spencer. A group of women are gathered around Madam Crimson. She's telling them stories of her travels, her visits with angels, and the energy they passed to her.

Ms. Eldridge watches this from the doorway, finally stepping forward and interrupting her speech.

"Good morning, all!" Ms. Eldridge announces. "I

must deliver some difficult news. It seems we have a fraud among us."

Mr. Spencer glares at me. My body feels numb and I try to speak to him through my eyes.

I didn't tell her anything. Please believe me.

John's nowhere to be seen. If we're going to run, we need to be together.

Ms. Eldridge scans the room slowly. She pauses on Mr. Spencer, as if waiting for a reaction, then continues on.

"Madam Crimson."

The large woman smiles, pushing herself up from her seat. Her jewelry clanks together.

Ms. Eldridge walks beside her and lays a hand on her arm.

"I had my suspicions about you and took it upon myself to investigate your cabinet last night when you were out in the yard with the others."

Madam Crimson tries to pull away, but Ms. Eldridge's hand has tightened, like a trap that's sprung.

"This woman doesn't speak to the spirits. She speaks through this," Ms. Eldridge says, ripping a small rubber hose from Madam Crimson's sleeve. As she continues to pull, we all see that the hose runs down her dress and under the carpet, hidden by the flowing fabric and jingling jewelry.

"When the lights are off, she sticks this in the end of the trumpet"—Ms. Eldridge pulls at the hose, following it to the back of the cabinet, where there's a small mouthpiece—"then crouches here to make the sounds you hear."

Madam Crimson clucks at this, but the crowd stands, eerily silent.

"Before the lights come on"—Ms. Eldridge says, tugging the end of the hose so it falls from the trumpet and slithers under the cabinet—"she hides the evidence, hoping she's fooled you."

There's a gasp from the crowd, and Madam Crimson backs away.

"She's a fraud," Ms. Eldridge says.

A woman in the crowd raises her fist and yells, "Fraud!" and then a chant starts, small at first, and then getting louder as men and women join in.

"Fraud, fraud, fraud," they chant.

Clenched fists pound at the air, beating imaginary drums.

Fraud, fraud, fraud.

The group closes in, surrounding her. Madam Crimson stands, grabbing some of her things before they force her out of the room, down the hall, and out the front door into the yard.

I'm caught in the stampede of angry people.

Shadows dance on the walls, dark black things from the harsh morning light. These aren't like the ones I saw last night though; these are connected to people, waving their arms.

Fraud, fraud, fraud.

The sound is almost a scream now, and Madam Crimson stumbles down the front steps and falls onto the cobblestones of the courtyard.

There's no time to hear her side of the story, no trial with witnesses, no defense. The decision has been made, the punishment given.

"A curse on you all!" she screams, just as two men throw her cabinet on the ground. The wood cracks on impact, spilling out trumpets and silks and pamphlets.

"Stop it!" Charles commands, helping her to her feet. He points to two men and says, "Load her tricks into the carriage. Everyone back!"

The men obey, and Charles guides her to the horses.

The chant continues, softer now. *Fraud, fraud, fraud.*

"I'll take you into town," he says. "You can figure out the rest on your own."

Madam Crimson stands, pleading, "Listen . . . all of you . . . you must understand . . ."

Her faraway accent is gone, and the New York

sounds slip out. "I'm not a fraud. I'm not! It can all be explained if . . ."

But no one is interested in hearing her side. They push her toward the carriage, still chanting, and she hoists herself up, sticks out her tongue at them. Charles hops into the front and whips the reins, and the horses speed from the house, onto that well-worn dirt road.

Mr. Spencer runs behind, holds a fist in the air and yells, "And never come back!"

He's smiling, though, that stupid nasty smile.

John watches it all from the porch, leaning against the railing. His eyes search for mine.

When all the others return inside, I stay on the porch, keeping enough distance from him that it doesn't appear that we're together.

"We need to be more careful," John whispers. "If he gets caught, so do we."

He's right, and I know Mr. Spencer is thinking the same thing. I can see it on his face.

I slip back inside the house, grab the box of photographic plates from the table, and clutch them under my arm.

I won't let us get caught.

A Sign in the Night

The crowd breaks into groups later that day, and Mr. Spencer takes more pictures, pulling from the plates I've marked with the wax signal. He cuts the session short when he's used up all of the ones I've worked on and collapses into a chair.

"That's it for now," he says, looking at me with a flash of disgust for not finishing more last night. "My energy is spent."

The group returns upstairs, joining others in the parlor or out in the yard around the tree.

I sit on the porch and watch them, noticing a broken piece of wood from Madam Crimson's cabinet on the cobblestones, and the memory of her being chased from the Society plays over and over in my mind, horrible chants still echoing in the air.

Mr. Spencer stumbles out of the front door and covers his hand with his mouth. He whispers, "Why didn't you finish them all?"

I consider telling him what I saw last night and

what Ms. Eldridge told me, but decide against it. He wouldn't believe me. And with each passing hour, I'm not sure I believe it myself.

It was just a storm, an easy fact instead of superstition.

"Do it tonight," he hisses, and I nod, looking away from him to the trees at the top of the valley.

"And get rid of any evidence. We can't be sloppy."

He's right of course. I know it.

That night, when all the guests have settled in, the rest of the plates are waiting for me in my room. I should do what Mr. Spencer says and finish them, but I can't bring myself to. I'm exhausted. I curl up in bed and I feel like I'm treading water in the middle of the ocean, bobbing up and down, dipping beneath the surface into uneasy sleep before bursting up for air. My heart races. My dreams are full of bright light and moving shadows. I feel like I'm losing my mind, my sense of what's real.

It's all pretend. Everything's a lie. You didn't see anything last night. The shadows were in your mind.

A light flashes across my wall. Am I still dreaming? It flashes again. And again.

Flash. Flash.

Peering out the window, I see a small pinprick of light from the trees. On and off. On and off.

Wait . . . flashlight, I remember George telling me in the barn. Has he come to see me?

I pull on my dress and shoes and head outside. The ground is cold, and the air stings my lungs. Still, the light flashes off and on, and I climb the wall and follow the field up a hill and to a row of trees that leads to the woods.

When I get close to the source of the light, I whisper, "George?" but there's no answer. "Is that you, George?"

Only the wind replies, rustling the leaves on the ground.

"Where are—"

Suddenly he appears, jumping from his spot and making a sound like a ghost.

I cover my mouth, trying not to scream.

"So, you *are* real," he says, flicking the flashlight's button again.

"Course I am."

"You told me you were a ghost, and I started to think I dreamed you up."

"Was I a good dream or a bad dream?"

"Not either of the two, just a dream," he says, shining the light toward the Society. "It's bigger than I expected."

I push his hand away.

"Careful with that light. Someone might see it."

"It's a creepy-looking house," he says warily.

"You don't know the half of it."

Should I tell him about the shadows, how they grabbed John's arms and pulled him down the aisle of the assembly hall? No. I told George my brother was dead, and I need to keep my stories straight. He doesn't seem like the kind of boy that can keep his mouth shut.

"What are you doing out here in the middle of the night?"

He laughs.

"It ain't nighttime for a farmer. It's early morning for me. Sun'll be up soon. Pa's gone into town and I always get up early for the cows. Thought I'd slip over here first."

"How'd you know I'd see your light?"

"Didn't know for sure. Was just hoping to see the place. What's it like there?"

I stare at him.

"Come on. Tell me, Liza. Or was it Violet?"

A shiver runs through my body at the mention of my mother's name, but then I remember that's what I told him at our first meeting.

"It's Liza, actually. I lied to you. I'm sorry."

"It's all right. I figured as much, you being a runaway and all."

"I'm not a runaway, either," I say. "I'm sorry, George, I lie a lot."

"Well, gosh, I reckon we all do. But if you're not a

runaway, where are your parents?"

"They're gone," I whisper. "I live with my uncle now. He's down at the Society."

Why am I telling him the truth? I shouldn't have said that. I consider telling him that that was a lie, too, but he interrupts my thoughts.

"So, what's it like there?"

"Spooky," I say, trying to sound dead serious. "There's ghosts everywhere. I've seen demons in the halls, angels in the outhouses. We eat squirrels for breakfast and—"

"Very funny," George says. "Have you talked to your parents on the other side?"

He asks it so earnestly that it makes me stop joking.

"No," I say. "Not yet."

"I'm sorry. I shouldn't have asked."

"You need to leave, George. It's not—"

"Do you see that?" he asks. He blinks the flashlight once more at the Silver Star Society, and in the darkness, I see the shapes moving down the hill and around the yard, those smokelike shadows made of the darkest black, rising from the ground and circling the house.

There are things only children can see, Ms. Eldridge said.

"Do you see them too?" I ask.

"Them?" he asks, and the moon moves from behind the clouds and the shadows seem to retreat. I see now he wasn't looking at the same thing.

He points to the front door. A person staggers into the yard.

"Who'd be out this early?" he asks.

"*We* are, George."

George places his thumb on the flashlight button, and I swat it away.

"Hey, I want to see who it is."

"You can't use the light."

I can tell it's Mr. Spencer by the way he walks. He hobbles out the front gate and creeps along the wall, looking left and right and then back at the house. He's holding a shovel and clutching something to his chest, but I can't see what it is from this far away. Suddenly, he starts to run, looking back at the house as he scales the hill that leads to the woods.

Get rid of any evidence, he told me earlier. *We can't be sloppy.*

Is that what he's doing? But what does he have to hide? I'm the one with secrets, all of them stashed in my Hidden Place or buried deep in my mind.

What would he do if he saw me out here, let alone with someone else?

"I have to go," I say. "Come back again and I'll tell you a secret."

"What is it?"

I don't know what I'll tell him. I have too many to choose from, but it's the only way I can get him to leave.

"It wouldn't be a secret if I told you."

George nods, intrigued by my offer.

"All right. I'll sneak away next time my dad's in town. I promise," he says. He turns around and heads into the trees, vanishing into the branches.

I check the hill for Mr. Spencer and then creep back toward the house. When I arrive at the stone wall, I wrap my fingers around the edge and peek over. The smoky shadows are gone, if they were ever there at all. It was probably just the moon reflecting off the fog. Fox walks from the cemetery and sits, staring at me.

Don't bark, girl. Please don't bark.

She wags her tail, and I kick off from the ground, wrapping my legs over the top of the wall and sliding down. A chill passes through my body as I land on the frosted grass. The air feels thin. It's quiet in the yard, but I hear the soft scrape of metal against dirt as Mr. Spencer shovels.

I squint over the wall. His outline moves beside a large rock, ten feet into the woods, pushing the shovel down with his foot and pulling up a heap of dirt.

I can't let him see me. I run back into the basement door and crash into my bed.

The rest of the plates can wait. I count my breaths, hoping to fall asleep, praying the shadows don't break into the house and grab John in his sleep.

Are you still there? I think, wishing he could answer me with his mind, but of course he doesn't reply.

SAVE FOREVER

I sleep until morning, never working on the rest of the plates. Mr. Spencer will be mad, but I don't care. I needed the rest.

At breakfast, I carry the box of photographic plates with me. Maybe I can drop them on the ground, shatter them into a million pieces. That would make a good excuse.

Mr. Spencer looks at me and I shake my head. He sneers and stands, makes a big show of coughing into his hands.

"I'm not feeling well," he announces, heading to the stairs. "Perhaps I'd better stay in my room today."

A few people grumble. First the assembly hall is closed and now this, but it's not my fault. I couldn't bring myself to make the ghosts last night, not after everything that's happened.

Charles comes beside me and taps the package of plates.

"This changes our plans," he says. "Our new order of supplies should be in soon. Once it arrives, we'll have plenty more plates to use. And if you're going to be my assistant, you'll need to learn how this works. Wait here."

He goes down to the basement and returns with his camera and tripod, then pulls out one of the unaltered plates from the top, covering it in a cloth and placing it into the wooden plate holder before sliding it into the back of the camera.

"Have you ever taken a picture?" he asks, and I shake my head. Another lie, stacked on a pile of them. He waves at me to follow and we go out into the yard, standing in the stone courtyard. He extends a hand as if offering the entire world to me as a gift and says, "What would you like to save forever?"

I've never thought of it that way before. *Save forever.*

Spinning in place, I take in the scenes around me. In the late morning light everything looks bright and beautiful—the hill leading to the woods, the moss in between the stones in the wall, the way the sun reflects off the top of the gravestones. John is watching us from the porch, and I want another picture of me and him together, but I don't dare ask for that. People would wonder why.

I keep looking. Even the house is beautiful with its white bricks and green railings wrapping around the porch. Will I want to remember this place? I doubt it. We'll either be kicked out or leave on our own, but by the time we're at stop number twenty, I'll try to forget everything about it.

Then an idea hits me so strong I can't believe I had to think at all.

"You," I finally say. "I want a picture of you."

Charles looks surprised and shakes his head.

"No, there must be something—"

"I want a picture of you," I say, a little more forceful this time. He's shown me kindness and I want to remember that, even if it will end on some day with chants of *fraud*. He'll think I'm terrible then, joining in the chants, driving us away. This, before all that eventually happens, is the moment I want to save.

He rubs the back of his head and looks at me in amusement. "Well, I did say you could pick anything, didn't I? Where would you like me to stand?" he asks, and then motions at me to follow. "Come, let's search for good light."

We walk around the yard, stopping at a thin maple tree behind the chapel. The branches are bare mostly, save for a few dried leaves that haven't fallen from the autumn winds. Still, it's a beautiful thing in its own twisted way, and the sun paints spots of light on its trunk.

"What about here?" Charles asks, propping his hand on the bark.

"Yes," I say. "There."

He sets up the tripod and attaches the camera, eyeing up the shot through the little viewfinder, then waves me over. We don't need the flash outside in this light, and I'm grateful for that. The powder and explosions still startle me, and would remind me of what happened in the assembly hall, too.

"You focus like this," he says, twisting the lens. He adjusts the exposure and rests his finger on a button. "This is the *shutter*. Press it when you're ready. Understand?"

I nod, approaching the camera like it's strange to me.

Charles runs to the tree. Its branches look like wings growing from his back, and the field behind him is spotted with gravestones.

"Whenever you're ready," he says, sliding his hand into his pocket. There's a small smile on his face and his eyes are warm and welcoming.

Charles stands, frozen, waiting for the lens to gather the light and form the image, saving it forever on the glass.

I frame the shot, squinting through the viewfinder.

Everything appears small and distorted through the little glass lens.

There's movement behind him. At first I think it's just the wind, maybe leaves blowing or a small flock of birds, but then I see the shape of a head sloping down into shoulder, those pale white eyes and cotton-stranded hair.

Something's coming toward him. Or *someone*. It looks like one of those shadows, but in the daytime, it's so faint that it's barely a shimmer.

I want to call out, warn him to be careful, that those things are dangerous. They'll grab him, pull him to the light, try to take him to the other side.

My hands tense in panic and—

Click.

I look up, ready to yell, but nothing is behind him and the exposure is done. My mouth is still open, the warning perched on my lips, but I swallow it down. I imagined it. It was spots in my eyes, those dark things that float in my vision when the sun is bright.

I emerge from behind the camera, and Charles claps his hands and says, "Let's see how it turned out."

We walk through the snaking halls of the house to the darkroom. He switches on the red bulb, pours the chemicals, and begins to work. When the image begins to forms, it's a negative of what I saw with my eyes, everything in reverse. The bright sky is dark and the dark branches are almost white. I watch as the features on Charles's face takes shape, rising from nothing.

"I can't remember the last time I've had a photograph of me," Charles says, leaning down to look at the image. He picks it up to examine. "In fact, I—"

All of a sudden, he drops the plate into the tray of liquid as if it's burning his fingers.

"Liza," he whispers, and he looks at me in wonder, the red from the light reflecting off his glasses like little spots of fire.

He points at the plate. Behind the image of him and the tree, a figure stands between the gravestones, the ghostly shape of a woman rising in the glass.

"A spirit."

"No," I say.

"*Look.*"

Charles traces his finger around the shape. It's in the same spot as the shimmer I saw, its faint white eyes focused on me.

"It can't be a spirit. It's not—"

I search for another explanation, anything that will make sense. Did I forget to mark one of the plates I worked on? I must have. That's the only way this could have happened. They were never out of my sight, even for a—

Wait. No. That's not true.

I left them on the table at breakfast yesterday, and they were there when I returned . . . but who else could have changed them?

John was in the dining room. It couldn't be him, even though he knows my methods and has a better eye for spirits.

Mr. Spencer? I wasn't gone long enough for him to take the plates, alter them, and return them to the table. Besides, his work was never this good. And this work *is* good—the best I've ever seen. My ghosts never looked this real. I could never make them look like they were in motion, could never make their bodies seem to fade as their legs approached the ground. Cotton is much too difficult to work with to make something like *that*.

Others could be tricked into believing this is just like the photographs we've made, but I know better. I know the truth—this is different.

"You have the gift too," Charles whispers, snapping me back to the moment.

"I don't have the gift," I say, and a cry gets caught in my throat.

"It's all right, Liza. It's nothing to be scared of."

"I'm not scared. I don't believe it."

I shouldn't say that, but I have to.

"I didn't, either. But now I have faith. If it wasn't real, how else could we explain this?" Charles asks as he gestures to the plate.

No. It's not real. I tell myself that over and over. Someone is doing this to me. Or I forgot and I'll find the same face cut from newsprint in my Hidden Place.

Charles looks at me and smiles. Why did he ask me

to take a picture? Was it him? Maybe *he* did it as a way to catch me in my lies. But how could he know I would take a picture of him? And what was it I saw behind him?

If he gets caught, so do we, John said.

I grab the side of the table and lean over the tray, taking in the thin outline of the woman behind the tree. I study the blur of her dress. The way she stares at the camera, it almost seems like she wanted to be seen, like she was hoping I would capture her.

"Let's find Ms. Eldridge. Quickly," Charles says. He covers the tray with a cloth, allowing it to finish developing, and we walk through the house. How will I tell Mr. Spencer what's happened?

"Ms. Eldridge!" Charles calls, and she answers from the parlor. "You must see this! Come quickly!"

Ms. Eldridge follows us through the house and into the little darkroom and squints over the tray, clucking her tongue when she sees the shape on the glass.

"Well!" she says. "It seems our little mystery grows. This is quite an image, dear. Do you know her?"

"No," I say, truthfully.

She leans over the image and squints.

"And you, Charles?"

Charles shakes his head.

"No, ma'am. Doesn't look familiar."

"So what should we do about this?" Ms. Eldridge asks, with a twinkle in her eye. "If the guests find out about *your* gift, they'll line up for you faster than they would for that Spencer character. It's up to you. Do you hide your gift or share it with the others?"

"No, please. You can't tell anyone."

She stares at me for a long time, choosing her words carefully.

"If that is what you want. This will stay between the three of us."

And just like that, she grabs the plate from the liquid and opens the door, holding it up to the light and destroying the image.

"There," she says. "It's gone."

As soon as she leaves, I run out of the darkroom and down the basement stairs to my bedroom and lean against the door, then open the suitcase and pry open the compartment to my Hidden Place. Tears stream down my face. How did this happen? I pull out the cotton strands, the stack of papers, the cut-out faces, flipping through them to see if any of the faces could be mistaken for the woman in the photograph.

Not this one. Not this one, either.

Please make sense, I pray, but none of the photos look anything like that woman in the photograph.

I try to remember how the woman looked,

standing behind Charles and the tree. It's only been destroyed for a few moments, but I already feel the memory of it changing to something more ordinary, made of paper and cotton.

If I could just look at the plate again, I'd see the truth. It must be one that I created. The plates got scrambled and we used one that I had changed.

Yes. That's it.

But then I wonder, is my mind just shifting things around, making up a reality that forms around the one I want to be true?

The earth seems to rock under my feet and I lie on the bed. I need more sleep. I tried last night but didn't get enough. That's all it is. Tonight, I promise myself I will.

What would John think if I told him what I saw? That they're playing a trick on me? He saw the shadows in the assembly hall, felt their arms around him. Would he believe it?

I put everything back in my Hidden Place and lock my suitcase. When I open the door, Charles is standing there, waiting for me.

"What's wrong?"

"Nothing," I say, sidestepping him and racing up the stairs.

John is sitting on a bench in the front hallway, leaning his head against the wall, the little cowlick stuck on a seam of wallpaper. I reach out my hand and fix it, quickly, before anyone sees.

There's no one around, and Charles is still in the basement, so I whisper it fast, before I change my mind.

"Something terrible has happened. I took a picture and one of the shadows was in it. It looked like—"

"The shadows?" he asks.

"Those things we saw in the assembly hall."

He squints at me, like he's not understanding. I glance at the door to the basement, listen for Charles's footsteps.

"You saw them too. Tell me you remember the shadows."

He lifts his eyebrows, signaling me to be quiet.

Mr. Spencer coughs and staggers down the stairs. He's still pretending he's sick, but the smell of his drink wafts off him. Even in his state he can tell something is wrong by my red and blotchy eyes.

"Come with me," he says, motioning to the parlor. It's empty now, and he grabs my wrist and pulls me in.

"You better have a good reason for not doing your job," he slurs.

"Did you change one of my plates?" I ask.

He releases his grip, startled by my question.

"What are you . . . did *I*?"

For a moment, I consider telling him what

happened today, but don't. He'd take his anger out on me.

"What were you doing outside last night?" I ask, and he stares at me, surprised I knew that.

"How did you—"

"You were burying something."

"Were you *following* me?"

"I could hear it from my room," I lie.

He looks worried and checks the hallway outside the room to make sure no one can hear us.

"I was hiding evidence just like I said," he hisses. "And you'd do well to hide *yours*, too."

"We need to leave," I say. "Something's not right here. I can feel it."

"The only thing *not right* is you, Liza. Without the plates finished I can't take pictures. Without pictures I can't make money and without money—"

"Don't take it out on John," I whisper.

"*John*," he spits and raises a hand, about to bring it down, but I twist out of his grip and run outside to the yard where I'm safe from him, where plenty of people can see me.

I run out to the maple tree and hide behind it. I rub my foot along the stone wall, feel the tingle in my toes. There are no shadows out now, and the memory of that woman in the photograph changes again. In my mind, I can almost see the cut marks around the paper now, the spots where the cotton curls around.

You forgot to mark a plate. That's all it is. Relax.

When dinnertime comes, I'm not hungry. I take a few bites and sneak the rest to Fox.

The house is quiet this evening. Guests are outside, and it's unusually warm for autumn, a last small burst of summer. The sun is low in the sky and the clouds are so colorful that they look like the heavens have opened up.

When it's dark, I work through the rest of the plates, just as Mr. Spencer commanded, cutting out the faces as quickly as I can. The edges are rough and the cotton bodies are sloppy, but I don't care. I can't look at these anymore. I just need to finish.

I set my creations on the black board, arrange my lantern.

Click. Click. Click.

As soon as I'm done, I stuff the scraps into my Hidden Place. Is it safe there? Or should I hide the evidence better, like Mr. Spencer did in the woods?

When I crawl into bed and shut my eyes, I can see Mother and Father in the yard of our old house, the sun high in the sky and illuminating them. They're trying to tell me something but I can't hear it. I try to walk to them, run, but I can never get close enough.

Sleep finally comes, washing over me, and ghostly figures blend into the corners of my dreams.

MEMORIES

When I wake the next morning, my head feels clear for the first time in ages, and I run upstairs and out the door to the courtyard. The sky is blue and massive, without a cloud in sight and the air is crisp and smells like smoke and cooked grease. Brown leaves are strewn about the yard and blow out onto the road. This morning, in the light, I see this place for what it is—a normal house filled with normal people. The thought of mysterious shadows slinking along the lawn might have made sense to my tired mind, but they seem ridiculous now.

Maybe it was the darkroom chemicals. Or all the travel. Any number of things.

I push those things down, seal them tight in the Hidden Place of my mind.

Days pass quickly here. Each morning, Ms. Eldridge reads out the schedule of events and posts them on a wooden board in the entryway. There are physical readings inside the house, group spiritual paintings in the parlor, and prayer circles in the front yard. On some afternoons there are classes on spirit knocking frauds, where mediums summon tapping sounds from the dead. On others there are slate readings in the dining room that leave mysterious chalk marks on a board.

While Charles and some of the guests work to repair the damage to the assembly hall, Ms. Eldridge has her daily session in the front yard to connect with Annabelle, but I don't go. Even though it's outside, I don't want to see the shadows or that strange light again, to have the buzzing in my head and feel like I have no control. I'm just starting to convince myself it never happened.

Each morning, once the guests have scattered, John and I meet on the porch. When no one is around, we talk about our parents, remembering our old home, the way the rooms smelled in the winter, how the bugs swarmed around the pond and the little minnows swam at the edges. We talk about picking berries and eating corn on the front porch, summer days spent at the nearby lake, swinging from tree branches and splashing into sludgy water. My memories are all baked in sunlight, perfect things that I don't want dulled by truth.

"Do you remember the first time we met Mr. Spencer?" John asks.

I think back to that day in the courthouse, after everything happened and we were given to him.

I shiver.

"Of course I do. It was awful."

"No, the *first* time," he says.

I don't answer.

"He visited us that summer before Mother and Father got sick."

I pause. "No he didn't."

"He had his camera and they buyed a portrait of us. We sat out on the front steps."

I stare at him, waiting to see if he's joking.

"They *bought* us a portrait. And that never happened, John. Anyway, you're younger than me. How do you even remember if I can't?"

"I just do."

Charles said a picture was like saving something forever, and if that's true, there's nothing I wouldn't give to go back to that moment. I try to imagine my whole family on the porch, sitting while Mr. Spencer set up his tripod and camera. In my mind, his finger hovers over the shutter and—

Click.

The picture doesn't form.

"I think you imagined that."

He shrugs.

"Maybe. Or maybe you just forgot."

"No," I say, because if I forgot that, what other memories have I lost? Memories are all I have.

People come and go throughout the week at the Society. At any given time, a carriage is being hitched or unhitched, or a car is being loaded or unloaded. It's easy to blend into the scenery, get lost in the motion. Sometimes, I feel like I'm one of the ghosts in my pictures, caught in a blur, never really seen. I eat food at the planned times, then go to my room as soon as the sun sets. I don't want to see those strange shadows again. If they're real, I want to pretend they're not. Is that so wrong?

Here at the Society, Mr. Spencer enjoys his role as the mysterious stranger with a special gift. Everywhere he goes, people surround him, asking questions about the spirits he captures. From the hall, I watch him play cards in the living room with other men, hypnotizing them with his stories. It's easy to get drawn in, to start believing what he says.

Later, he leads groups of people down into the basement, and Charles helps him set up the camera in the center room, opening the door to let in the light.

"Whose turn is it today?" Mr. Spencer asks.

The first subject is a woman whose husband died last year. She stares into the camera lens, determined to see him again.

Click.

A man is next, with another story of loss.

Click.

A parade of sorrow moves through, and when we use up what is left of the photographic plates, a list is made of who will be next when our order arrives in town. Charles carries the plates up to the small darkroom beneath the stairs. He's quiet, pointing at bottles and mumbling at me to place them on the table. He works quickly, mixing the chemicals in trays, exposing the plates, absorbed in his work.

The finished photographs hang on a string along the rafters of the basement like trophies that prove Mr. Spencer's gift. Guests look at each one, inspecting the outlines of the spirits behind each person, whispering their amazement. I'm drawn to the picture of the first woman Mr. Spencer photographed today, with her striking eyes and firm expression. The face of a man hovers beside her, blurred just enough to see a small smile on his lips, like he has a secret. I wonder if the man looks enough like her husband to fool her, and my stomach twists at the thought of my deception.

You're a wicked thing.

When the pictures are all hung, Charles kneels before me. He seems to see the hurt in my eyes and hugs me.

"Thank you for your help, Liza."

I hug him back, and soon tears are pouring down my face. He's been so kind to me and I don't deserve it. Not after what I've done.

The next morning, Charles waves to me from the porch.

"Ah, there you are!" he says. "I've received word from Mr. Muller. Our order of supplies has arrived, and I'm heading into town. Come with me."

I follow him to the carriage and we ride off, up the hill and through the narrow tunnel of trees.

Soon, the town comes into view, dark squares of brick and stone in the middle of large fields of yellow-green grass.

The sky is bright, but there are a few dark clouds far in the distance.

Charles steers the carriage through the main road in town and then turns a corner into the alley. He hitches the horses and enters the shop through the back door, just like last time.

Mr. Muller is sweeping the floor and grins when he sees us.

"Ah, Charles, my boy! You got my message."

"Yes, sir."

"Still have your *helper* with you?" he asks, but there's something about the way he says the word that I don't like.

"Were you able to get the supplies?"

"Indeed," Mr. Muller says, moving his hefty frame behind the counter and lifting two boxes. They're filled with plates and paper and chemicals, more than I've ever seen together at one time. "This is all I could get. Hard to come by, and they're getting expensive. If you want more, I'll need full payment up front."

"When have I ever not been good for it?" Charles asks, removing an envelope from his breast pocket and counting out the bills.

"Look what else I have," Mr. Muller says with a grin, opening a box that reveals dozens of bottles filled with brown liquid.

Charles peers at the contents and sniffs. "I believe that's illegal, sir."

"Only the sale and transportation, dear boy. But I didn't say how they got here. And I didn't offer any to *you*, did I?" Mr. Muller sneers.

"I suppose not."

Charles tucks the package under his arm and motions at me to leave. Just as we're almost through the door, Mr. Muller hits his fist to the table.

"Oh, Charles, I wanted to ask—where did you say that girl came from?"

I look to the ground and Charles steps in front of me.

"I didn't say."

"I see. There was a man with some questions that stopped by recently. He asked if I saw a young girl about her age traveling around with an older fellow."

A chill races through my body, and I feel my heartbeat thump all the way in my ears.

"He must have been talking about someone else," Charles says, patting my shoulder and guiding me to the back door.

"Good. Well, I didn't tell him about the Loony Star," Mr. Muller says with a chuckle. "But I got the sense he was already heading there."

I can hardly breathe and seem to float from the store and back into the alley and into the carriage. I can't feel my arms or legs. I hope my face doesn't show it.

Don't look at me, Charles. Please don't look.

"I wonder what that was about," Charles says, but I can't answer. If I talk, he'll know something is wrong. He'll hear it in my voice.

A man with some questions.

Maybe it's nothing. Maybe just a coincidence, but in my heart, I know it must be the detective from New York. He's followed us here. I think back to the way that man looked in the alley behind our house in Rochester, cupping his hands around his eyes to peer into our room. I had seen him for a moment the previous day, but that night, only the harsh angles of his face were lit by the yellow streetlights, and he seemed different, like he had disguised himself before. Would I recognize him if I saw him at the Society? Would he remember me and John?

When we return, I go inside, enter one of the small doors that leads to a narrow passageway hidden between the rooms. It circles the edge of the house, and through the small spaces between the boards I can see a group of people gather in the front yard. Some of them are familiar, and some are new. If the man was at Mr. Muller's store recently, that means he may have just arrived at the Society. But new guests come here every day, and I'm not sure I can tell them apart. I should have paid better attention. I should have been more careful.

I look at faces. There's a man about the same height as the detective with a big beard and wire glasses. Could that be him? There's a couple by the courtyard that I never saw before. Did he bring his wife or hire someone to play the part? What about that man in the ratty, old hat? He even wears it inside, almost like it's a disguise.

I search my memories, but they're jumbled and hiding from me.

I don't know, I just don't know.

Charles carries the boxes in from the carriage and sets them in the front hallway.

"Liza?" he calls, and I slink from the passageway and return. "Where'd you run off to?"

"Nowhere."

"Grab one of these."

I help carry the boxes of photographic plates down to the basement and we stack them in the corner.

"Keep a good lookout," he says with a smile. "Don't let anyone touch them."

"Of course."

I skip dinner that night, staying hidden away in my room. If the man is already here, maybe he'll give up and leave.

Or maybe he's already seen you and is waiting for his moment.

I have to hope he hasn't.

Later that night, when the house is settled, I hear creaking on the stairs, a slow whine as someone eases their weight from step to step, trying to be quiet.

Could that be him? Is he coming for me?

I curl into my blankets, lifting the corner so I can peek out.

Mr. Spencer walks through my doorway and produces a stack of newspaper clippings from under his arm. He throws them to the ground, fresh faces for me to choose from.

"New order from town? You have a lot of work ahead of you," he says, looking at the stacks of boxes.

He turns to head back to the stairs.

"Wait. Mr. Spencer, I—"

I want to tell him what Mr. Muller said, but can't bring myself to say it.

"What now?" he snarls.

"Nothing, sir. I'll start right away."

He nods, and once I hear his feet on the steps, I flip the newspapers, examining the faces he's selected. They're plain and featureless, easy to mistake for anyone.

I work through the night, marking the sides with drips of candle wax. I'll never get through them all today, will hardly even make a dent, and my ghostly pile of used cotton and paper faces grows.

In the early morning hours, a light appears in little bursts against my wall.

Flash flash flash flash.

George! He's come back to me. I jump up, but then stop—I promised him a secret. And I know exactly what I'll show him.

Get rid of any evidence, Mr. Spencer said. I ignored him for days, but I can't any longer, not with the detective possibly here. He was right, but first, I need someone to know the whole truth. No more lies.

I scoop up as much cotton and papers as I can hold and lift the beam to the back door, escaping into the cold air.

SECRETS IN THE NIGHT

I run to the stone wall, checking to see if the shadowy shapes are out tonight, but the yard is empty.

The icy grass is brittle under my feet and my breath trails in the air as I run toward the trees, drawn to the flashing light like a moth to a candle.

Wind howls across the valley, and a swirl of cotton blows from my arms and into the sky.

Clutching the scraps of my secret tight against my chest, I enter the shelter of trees.

Something moves through the branches, and there's a scratching sound on the ground.

"Over here," George whispers. He rubs his hands together and blows hot air into them. "I came back."

Suddenly, my mouth feels frozen, like the words are stuck on my tongue.

"Liza?"

I can't talk.

"What do you have?"

I stop for a moment, consider turning around and going back to my room, keeping everything locked in my Hidden Place forever. But if I do, I'll rot from the inside. I have to tell him. I have to let this out.

"A secret," I finally say, thrusting a finished picture toward him. It shows a woman with a ghost wrapped around her shoulders, and he holds the flashlight above it and blinks it on.

Flash.

The burst of light glows on the paper.

"What is—" he starts.

Flash.

"Is that—"

"A ghost," I say, but he hardly listens, continues flashing his light on the picture, running his fingers along the strange outline. "You remember back in the barn when you said all this spirit stuff is the work of the devil?"

"It's real," he whispers.

"If it is, then *I'm* the devil," I say.

He drops his flashlight and stares at me.

"What do you mean?"

"I made this. It's all fake."

Am I trying to convince him or myself of that?

"Golly," George says, and the word seems so out of place that I almost laugh. "How did—"

"Help me dig. I need to hide it," I say, setting a

rock over the stack of pictures and my supplies. The screams of *fraud, fraud, fraud* still bounce around my head, so I scratch at the ground, making a small hole with my fingers, scooping out clumps of dirt. George picks up the flashlight and comes beside me to help. His hands are rough, and he works fast without asking any more questions, and soon the hole is wide enough that I can stack all my supplies inside. I start to gather the pictures, but George shakes his head.

"Don't stop. It needs to be deeper," he says. "A good rain could wash this out."

He continues to work, breaking through the cold ground, throwing mounds of dirt beside us.

"Don't you want to know why we're hiding this?"

He stops and looks at me. "Figured you'd tell me if you wanted me to know. But you're my friend, so if you ask for my help, I'll give it."

My friend.

Tears well in my eyes and I look away.

"I do it for him," I say, handing him the picture of me and John, the one Mr. Spencer took as a test that first time we made the ghosts. The two of us stare into the camera, the shape of Mrs. Turner hovering above us.

George looks at it, confused, and finally, I decide to tell him the truth.

"This is my brother, John," I say. "When the

sickness came, it took our parents, and nearly took him, too. I promised them I would look after him, no matter what."

Suddenly everything is pouring out of my mouth, and it feels so good to finally tell someone. I tell him how John and I went to live with Mr. Spencer after our parents died, and how we started faking these awful pictures for money. I explain how a bit of cotton and a double exposure can make a ghost appear.

"It's a trick, it's all a rotten trick," I say, but it comes out like a cry. "I didn't know the lie would hurt people, but I do now, and I'm so sorry. I'm so sorry."

I'm talking fast, I know that, but I can't stop. I need it all out.

He stares at me throughout, not saying a word.

"Is your brother still alive? You told me he was dead."

"Course he is. That day I found you in the barn, he went with Mr. Spencer. I pretended to be a runaway and showed up later that night so they wouldn't suspect I was helping him."

"*Golly*," he says again, and flashes his light on the picture. "Well, that's a pretty good secret."

I force a smile.

"Do you think I'm evil?"

George is silent. He picks at the dried leaves around his feet and spins the flashlight in his other hand.

"You did what you had to do," he says, then he stands and shines the light into the hole. "I don't think it's right to trick people, but not sure I'd have done anything different if I was in your position."

I consider telling him about the light I've seen at the Society, and the shadows that pulled John toward it, but I don't know how to form the words. I should tell him about the picture of Charles, and the shimmering shape of the woman behind him. He'd never believe me. He'd think I was trying to trick him, especially after what I've just told him, and I'm still not sure I believe it myself.

But then, what was it I saw through the light? It seemed like a whole different world, a window through the thin place when the worlds of the living and the spirits crashed together.

He looks down the valley to the house.

"So, do you think *everyone* down there is a liar?"

"Of course they are, George. They're all just trying to steal money from people. This world is all there is."

"I don't believe that," George says, and he flashes the light again. The hole we've dug is deep enough now, so we start packing my supplies inside, then piling dirt on top, pressing it down with our hands so it's firm.

I don't bury the picture of John, can't bring myself to put it in the ground. I fold it in half and slip it into my dress. No one will find it if I always keep it with me.

"Why are we hiding this stuff now?"

"If they found this, they'd kick us out," I say. "The lady that runs the Society likes to expose frauds, even though I'm sure she's one too. We'd be marked wherever we went. You have to promise you won't tell anyone what I said."

George nods.

"I promise. But have you ever thought maybe they'd only kick *him* out and let you and John stay? You were only doing what he asked, and they wouldn't blame kids the same as adults."

"No," I say. It's true that of all the places we've been, the people here have been the kindest to me, but underneath it all, they're just like everyone else.

"You don't have to do this anymore," he says, stamping his foot on the mound of loose dirt, packing it into the hole. "You can stop if you want."

"No. You don't understand."

"Ma tells me sin is a choice, and lying is a sin."

I turn away from him. It was silly of me to think he'd understand, and suddenly I'm angry at him. He's not really my friend if he thinks that.

"Anyway, I need to go," he says. "Pa's in town for a few days, so I'll try to visit you again soon."

"Don't bother," I say. "Just live your perfect little life and forget I ever existed. I don't ever want to see you here again."

He frowns at me and shrugs, then runs through the trees, back toward his farm, and I'm alone in the woods again.

A tear slides down my cheek. I should have told him a fake secret. I shouldn't have told him the truth. I shouldn't have trusted him.

I run through the woods, passing the clearing where Annabelle is buried and head down the hill. Through my tears, shapes seem to follow me and move around the yard, floating across the courtyard.

Ignore them. Just ignore them and they'll go away.

I crawl over the stone wall and land in the yard. The shadows are everywhere, more than I've ever seen before. They glide around the house, their bodies wobbling through my tears.

They close in around me, and I can feel their hands around my wrists, their fingers tightening. I fall to the ground, and they pull me along the cold, wet grass.

I kick my limbs, scream out in my mind, but they don't let go. They pull me further, along the cobblestones, past the small square shape of the assembly hall.

I twist my body and arch my back, but there's too many, and their grip is strong.

The shadows lean over me and cover my mouth, and up close I can see their white eyes and lips. Some have white hair that blows in the wind like strands of cotton.

I'm dreaming. I'm only dreaming.

They continue to pull me, toward a single shadow waiting by the stone wall. It's a woman, I can see that from her shape, and in the moonlight, her white hair hangs below her shoulders.

I'm not imagining things. They are real. John saw them too, even if he won't admit it to me now.

It starts to rain, heavy and cold, and wind blows around us.

"What do you want?" I ask, and she holds out a hand.

"Where is he now?"

My ears buzz and a streak of light cuts in front of her, cracking through the night sky. The shadows release their grip on me and seem to walk back into the glow. They've led me here. Their job is done, but I don't know what they want me to see. The light is so bright I can hardly look at it. A golden field comes into view.

I rub my eyes and the woman comes into focus, her face soft and warm.

The spot begins to grow, like the air around us is splitting open. The edge spreads, wipes over the wall, and pieces of stone fall through, toward the other side where their rough surfaces are bathed in sunshine.

Behind her, I can see those shadowed forms that pulled me here, except they're different now. On the other side, the figures look like regular people, the tones of their bodies reversed, their eyes and hair just like mine. When they move, they are blurred and out of focus. I want to twist the lens, see them clearly, but I can't.

On this side, the sky is still dark. The rain gets harder, soaking me through, and the wind nearly knocks me to the ground. The tree in the front yard groans and a limb rips off and flies past me.

The light is a tear between our worlds, a doorway through the thin place.

The woman points toward the house, then raises her arms, fingers outstretched and wrapping around the firey edges of the glare.

"Stop it!" I yell. "Make it go away!"

"I can't for much longer," she says, her face contorting as she pulls the night sky together.

The edges touch, sparking, and for one last fleeting

moment I can see the grass and trees, the birds in the bright blue sky. It's only a glimpse, and it only lasts an instant before it disappears, like a camera flash exploding and then leaving nothing but the darkness.

The rain has stopped, and the wind is a whisper, moving through the grass.

A section of the wall has crumbled, destroyed by the light, and the large stones that fell through to the other side are gone, eaten up like the wooden boards in the assembly hall and the trees around Annabelle's grave.

Maybe I should run inside and grab John, leave this place before more damage is done, before the shadows find us, or the spot explodes and takes the whole house with it.

I stand, wipe the dirt from my clothes and run around the corner, staying in the darkness. A shape moves behind the house, but it's just a woman walking to an outhouse, wrapped in a blanket.

When she returns inside, I open the door to the basement and slip into my room.

George's voice repeats in my head.

You can stop if you want.

Can I?

The boxes of plates sit in the corner of my room, waiting for me to do my work.

George saw it so clearly, and I should have seen it,

too, after the crowd chased Madam Crimson from this place. This is the answer. This is the way to keep me and John safe. The ghosts will stop appearing in the pictures, and they'll know he's a fraud. If that's not enough, I'll tell the truth, scream it from the courtyard if I have to. We can leave this place, escape from the shadows, start a different life without the lies.

Ms. Eldridge and the Society will ruin our reputation, but is that so terrible? Mr. Spencer will have to take us somewhere else and find a different kind of work.

I relight the red candle, let the flame flicker until the wax is soft and mark all the plates in all the boxes, the ones I've changed and the ones I haven't.

When all of them are marked, I mix them up so that I can't change my mind later, then I hide in my bed, feeling like I've just lit the fuse on the bomb that will explode my life and everything around me.

THE EMPTY PLATES

I can hear the reaction to the wall's missing stones before I'm out of bed. The damaged spot is around the corner of the house, and I can't see it from the little window in my room. I imagine the guests are circling it now, feeling the places where the rocks were once stacked.

"Where do you reckon the stones went?" a man's voice asks.

"Toppled over in the wind," a woman replies.

"Well, where are they, then?"

I throw on a dress and walk upstairs, trying to look well-rested, like an innocent girl who's been in bed all night and couldn't possibly know what happened to the wall.

The shadows aren't the only problem I need to watch out for. If Mr. Muller was right, the detective is here, and he could be observing me right now, waiting to sneak up on me and—

"Good morning!" Charles says, rounding the corner with a plate of food.

He catches me looking out the window as the crowd of guests grows.

"Ah, I see you've seen this morning's excitement."

"What happened?" I ask, thinking it's a question an innocent person would have.

"Get some food and join me," he says, motioning to the dining room.

"I will," I say, but first, I search the rooms for John.

He's in the parlor. Fox is beside him, nuzzling her nose on his thin legs. I can't remember the last time I've seen him eat. I thought it would be good for him here, that being out in the fresh air instead of hidden in a back room would help his condition, but he's never looked worse, like this place is a bug that has latched on and is sucking the light from his eyes.

"What happened last night?" he asks.

I maneuver close, look out for Charles, and whisper, "Don't worry. We're going to leave soon."

"What do you mean?"

"I made a plan. You'll see. The shadows won't find us."

"Liza!" Charles calls from the dining room. "Where did you go?"

"Over here!"

I step to the window and pretend that I'm still looking out at the damage to the wall when he appears at the entrance to the parlor. I hope I'm far enough away from John that he doesn't suspect we were talking, but I'm not sure I care anymore.

"I fixed you a plate of food, after all," he says with a smile, and leads me back to the dining room. "It's getting cold."

Most of the guests are outside, so we eat our breakfasts in silence. Part of me expected that he would talk about the wall, give a theory as to how it happened, but, "It's a mystery," is all he said about it.

I like that he doesn't try to make something up, to tell me half-truths that will comfort me. He's content to let it be what it is.

"Have these things always happened here?"

"No," he says. "Only recently."

Once the daily schedules are posted and announcements are made in the front yard, I follow Charles to the basement. People have lined up for Mr. Spencer and he ushers a woman to the stool.

I keep an eye out for the detective. Every man that glances in my direction for a moment too long gets marked as a suspect in my mind. Some of them aren't the right size—too short or too tall or too wide, but I can't trust myself to know for certain. The glimpse I caught of him in the alley was brief.

It's dark in the basement. Scattered clouds have covered the midday sun and the door to the back yard is closed. It starts to rain, another one of those *sudden storms* that seems to have happened since I arrived.

"Don't move," Mr. Spencer says. "This flash will be loud and bright, but it's safe, I promise you. Keep your eyes on the lens."

He raises it in the air, and when he clicks the camera's shutter—*boom*—an electric current passes through the wire that leads to the flash and the powder explodes, bathing the woman on the stool in a brief wave of light. It fades as soon as it appears, blink and you'd miss it, and the woman stands and rejoins her partner.

"Who's next?" Mr. Spencer asks, pulling another plate that I've marked from the box. Is this one changed or empty? I mixed them up well, and it's a game of chance, impossible to know.

A man steps forward. He speaks of his mother who died from tuberculosis and Mr. Spencer makes a grand show about calling out to her, requesting her presence in the room. The man's about the same height as the detective, but looks a bit younger, and his hair is a dirty blond. What color was the detective's hair? I thought it was darker. Could it be? Maybe.

"Come beside him! Wrap your loving arms around him!" Mr. Spencer shrieks, his yellow teeth snapping as the man sits on the stool.

People move around the room, trying to get a better look. Shadows move as the shapes of the guests are lit by the bare electric bulbs mounted in the rafters and the oil lamps flickering on the walls. I try not to look at them. They're just ordinary shadows. That's all. Still, I wish I could see John, make sure he's all right, that none of them have broken free and grabbed him.

The wind howls outside, leaking in through the cracks around the doorframe. The photographs Charles developed tremble from the clothesline, as though the ghosts I created are trying to break free from the paper.

Mr. Spencer moves through the line, taking more pictures, the *boom* of the flash sending more shadows around the room, except they don't seem attached to the people anymore. They come from different angles and float on the walls, dark smudges that have untied themselves and are moving free.

Don't look. Don't look.

Mr. Spencer takes over a dozen portraits today, and each time he grabs a plate and slides it into the camera, I think about what might *not* be on the photograph when it's developed. Questions will start.

He'll think of some excuse, but once a seed of doubt is planted, it will grow.

That bomb is sitting in the camera, the fuse burning, getting shorter, working its way to an explosion in the darkroom.

When Mr. Spencer is finished, the guests move upstairs, and Charles waves me over to pack up the plates.

"Carry these up, please," he says. "I'll meet you there."

I pick up the box and look out the window. In the rain, someone moves past the glass.

For a horrible moment, I think it's the detective, but then I see its white eyes and hair, and the rain seems to bend around its body, making its whole outline shimmer in the yard, transparent enough that I can see the slope of the grassy hill through its chest.

No. No, not again.

They can't get us now. Not when we're so close to getting out of here.

I take Mr. Spencer's flash and pour a line of the gray powder into the top. It has a little trigger on the handle to detonate the flash if it's not connected to the camera, and I rest my finger on it, ready to pull.

I open the back door, step into the wet grass, hold the flash out as far away from my body as I can. I don't know what will happen if the powder gets wet, if it will still explode, so I run at the shadow, getting as close as I dare, and—

Boom!

—the flash explodes into a fireball, a plume of white smoke lifting off from it and floating into the sky until it disappears.

It smells awful, and wet chunks of powder have flown into the air and burned little spots down my arm.

A bolt of lightning hits the hill leading to the woods, and I wait to see if that tear of light appears.

Another shadow comes from behind me, and with my trembling hands, I fill the trough with more powder, using my body to shield it from the rain.

I pull the trigger—

Boom!

—and the shadow disappears into mist.

The wind howls. A shutter rips from the hinges beside one of the windows and flies from the house, and a piece of the roof follows.

Are John and I responsible for this? Charles said these storms only started recently, but he didn't say the words that I'm sure we were both thinking:

This only started once you came.

The door to the basement slams open and shut, open and shut, and the wood cracks.

I run back inside, put the bar back down, wedging it in place. I'll tell Charles it wasn't closed properly, that the wind caught it just right. He'll want to know why my clothes are soaked through, and I'll tell him I ran outside and tried to fix it. It's the only explanation I can give.

Charles is waiting for me, so I finish packing up the box and take the steps slowly, careful not to drop it.

John's standing at the top, and I'm so happy he's there and safe from the shadows that I hardly notice how angry he looks.

"You didn't change the plates," he whispers, but it's not a question. He can see it on my face, could probably read my thoughts as soon as I decided it. "That was your plan, wasn't it?"

"We can't talk here," I hiss. There's too many people around. I catch him in the corner of my eye as I walk past. "But get ready. We're leaving soon."

Behind me, a man about the same height as the detective is talking with his wife. His face is the kind that could look like anyone else. It's the kind of face I'd choose right away from a stack of pictures because if you squint your eyes and look at him out of focus, he could almost be anyone.

The man catches me staring and nods. I lift the box to hide my eyes. My stomach is twisting with nerves, and I nod at John to leave me.

I walk toward the darkroom, and the old man who recently arrived comes behind us and places a hand on my shoulder. He nods at the box.

"Need a hand?"

"No, sir. I'm not supposed to let these out of my sight."

"I see. It's a remarkable thing, isn't it?" he asks. "Spirits in photographs. Who'd have thought?"

He walks with a cane, his back curved at a painful angle, and his gray suit is old and ragged. His glasses are thick, and the right lens is fogged over.

"Are your parents here?" he asks.

"They're over there," I say, waving to a group of guests, and he nods.

I pull away from him and leave John, walking toward the darkroom. Charles is waiting beside Margaret, his fingers grazing hers, and when they see me, they pull apart.

"Ah, there you are!" he says, taking the box. His eyes widen when he sees my wet clothes and hair.

"Liza, what—"

"The door to the basement blew open. I had to run out and shut it."

He nods, accepting my answer.

"You should go change. Do you want to help me develop?"

"No. Not today."

He takes the box from me and enters the darkroom. Margaret leaves and I run down to my room to put on dry clothes. The rain has stopped for now, and sunlight is fighting its way through the clouds.

When I return to the hallway, John is there, sitting on the little bench beside the door to the darkroom.

I should tell him to leave, that we shouldn't be seen together, but what does it matter now?

"As long as we're together, everything will be fine," I say.

He wipes his eyes and hugs me.

"I'm not going anywhere, Liza."

"I know, John. You're staying with me."

A sharp whistle breaks the silence. Mr. Spencer stands at the end of the hallway, his lips curling. He walks forward, ignoring John and grabbing my ear.

"What are you doing?" he snarls.

I can see the anger in his eyes.

"Don't talk to him here, *ever*, do you understand?"

"No," I growl, and his eyes widen. I've never talked back to him before. "I'll talk to John wherever I want."

He pulls up on my ear. The pain shoots through my head and I see flashes of light.

"Let go of her!" John hisses.

"You're finished," I say, quiet enough that Charles won't hear from the darkroom.

"What did you say?" he asks.

"You're *finished*. I didn't work on the plates. I marked them with the wax, but they're empty. Now everyone will know you're a fraud, just like they already suspect you are."

Mr. Spencer releases me, and I fall against the wall, holding my ear with one hand, the pain beating through my head.

I should stay quiet, but I can't. I want to hurt him, and the words come spilling out.

"The plates were in my room," I spit. "Right next to my bed. I could have changed them, but I didn't."

He turns, heading toward the stairs.

"You're a stupid girl," he hisses, and maybe he's right.

"We leave now or I'll tell them everything. I'll show them the cotton and the newspapers in my suitcase," I say, but he doesn't answer. He runs to the stairs, taking them three at a time, getting ready to grab his things and run.

I look at the door to the darkroom. Inside, Charles is working on the plates. There will be nothing on the pictures, and people will start asking questions. I wait, ready for my moment, but when the door finally opens, Charles waves at me to join him in the darkroom.

"Look, Liza," he says. "They're the most beautiful yet."

I look at him quizzically as my eyes adjust to the red light. My jaw drops as I stare at the negatives, unable to believe what's in front of me. In the reverse image, guests sit on the stool, staring into the camera lens, and behind them are ghostly bodies, topped with a thin outline of a ghostly face. I think of those shadows moving around the basement, hit by the harsh light from Mr. Spencer's flash.

They're perfect, like the real spirit I captured in the photo of Charles.

What now? I think. *Can I still tell him the truth?*

In the darkness, Charles can't see my face. To him, this is just another stack of plates, another photographic miracle after dozens before. To me, it's a nightmare.

I move to the door, and Charles covers the trays, protecting the negatives.

"What's wrong?" he asks.

"Nothing," I whisper, then open the door, run down the hall. I need to find John.

I hear snippets of conversation as I pass the rooms. The sun has lost its battle with the clouds, and the wind and rain has started to pick up.

"More of those storms," a man says.

People lean to look out the windows.

The sky has turned a dark shade of green, and the sun is hidden behind clouds. The rain is falling harder.

"I fear the worst hasn't come yet," Margaret says. "Don't worry. Many storms have passed us by, and this house is still standing."

I barely listen, my mind too fixed on what I just saw.

I go down to my room and lean against the door, looking out into the yard at the rain clouds moving across the sky, the dark blotting out all the light.

A knocking sound comes from the stairs, boots on wood, and then there's a light tapping on my door.

"Open up," Mr. Spencer says, and I obey.

He smiles at me.

"Charles showed me the plates."

"I didn't change them. I don't know how—"

"You're lying again. What game are you playing at, Liza?"

"I just want to leave. We're in danger here. Everyone is . . ."

My voice fades away. I think of the light cracking through the sky and taking the boards from the assembly hall and the stones from the wall. What I want to say is, *Everyone is as long as we're here.*

"How can I trust anything you say?"

I don't know how to answer. I'm not sure I believe myself.

"Stop it," he says, pointing a finger in my face before leaving me. "All of this."

I stay in my room through the evening and into the night, buried under my blankets, staring up through my little window. A gentle rain splashes against it, and wind whistles throughout the house. The rain becomes a low growl.

I thought we'd be gone by now, screamed at, chased from this place, on our way to somewhere else.

Is this a normal rain, or something more? Is it like Ms. Eldridge said? Have the worlds of the living and the spirits crashed into each other?

I won't be able to convince Mr. Spencer of the danger. It sounds unbelievable to say it out loud.

It's time I stop waiting for things to happen to me. John and I can leave on our own. I'll hoist him on my back and run. We can hide in George's barn until I can steal some money and then make our own life together.

George.

Just thinking his name sends a pang of sadness through me. I wish I hadn't yelled at him. I wish he knew that I was sorry, that I didn't mean what I—

And just like magic, there's a *flash flash flash flash* against my wall, and when I look out my window, I see that small burst of light in the trees.

I can hardly believe it. After the terrible things I said, he's come back, just like he promised.

THE GIFT

I slip on my shoes and run outside, through the steady rain. My feet sink into the wet grass and mud as I scale the hill to the woods and enter the cover of trees. The crisscrossing limbs block out most of the rain, but the noise is still loud against the dried leaves, a constant wet rattle.

"Liza, over here!"

George signals me from his spot—*flash flash flash*.

"You came!" I yell, and run toward him, tears burning at the corners of my eyes.

"I'm sorry for what I said," George says. "I was wrong."

"No, you weren't," I whisper. "I think I knew you were right, and that's why I got so mad. I did what you told me to."

He stares at me, bug-eyed.

"So what happened?"

"I didn't change the plates, but the ghosts were still in the photographs."

"What?" he asks. "How?"

I wish I had an answer for him.

"I don't know, but it doesn't matter anymore. John and I are leaving," I tell him. "Can we stay in your barn? Just for a while."

He hesitates.

"I could ask my ma and pa, but—"

"No. Don't. Adults say no to everything, and there's no other choice. It's too dangerous for us to be here."

I don't tell him why. He wouldn't believe that I'm the cause of the tear in the thin place and the sudden storms, or the shadows stalking the valley. There'd be too much to explain, and I'm scared of the answer that's bubbling beneath the surface of my mind. The truth is there, fighting its way out of the Hidden Place of my mind.

George thinks for a moment, then says, "I can leave the beam over the door loose and you can shake it free. Pa will find you eventually, so you can only stay for a bit. I could try to talk to them, explain what's happened, but—"

I shake my head.

"We'll come tomorrow and hide in the straw until the storms pass, then we'll figure out what to do next."

George's parents won't let us stay, I know that

good and well, but we'll run before word gets back to the Silver Star Society. John and I will keep to ourselves, stay on our own, stealing what we need, never stopping long enough to get caught. It's the only way to keep him with me, safe from those shadows that want to take him.

"These storms are weird, coming and going all the time," George says, listening to the rain. "Pa says this one has the feeling of something big, so you'll have to move quick."

I look down in the valley. The rain is like a dark curtain whipping across the ground, and in the yard, a shape moves against the house. Not a ghost—a real flesh-and-blood person.

"Liza," George whispers, holding up the flashlight and pointing it at the house.

George's thumb slides onto the button of the flashlight. I swat it away.

I can tell it's a man, and for an instant, I think it might be Mr. Spencer, out again to hide evidence, but the shape is wrong.

The detective.

The man cups his hands around his eyes and peers into the window to my room. He doesn't seem bothered by the rain, treats it like it's a disguise to wrap around himself, saving him from seeing other people out in the yard. No one will be using the outhouse tonight—they'll stick to the chamber pots, stay in the warmth of their rooms.

I want to get a good look at him, see him clearly now so I know who to avoid when we run. Before George can protest, I grab his hand and move through the trees, leaping over a roaring stream and through a bank of twisting vines, leaving the woods at a different spot and running down the valley, pushing against the rain. The grass is slippery, and I try to stay low until I reach the stone wall. I can see the shape of the detective now, staring into my room, wiping the rain from the glass with the sleeve of his shirt. Somewhere deep in the woods, a tree cracks and falls and the noise makes him jump. His head turns, and lightning rips through the sky, reflecting off the lenses of his glasses.

I feel like I'm back in that alleyway with John, watching his silhouette, waiting for him to leave before sneaking back into the house. Except this time, I won't tell Mr. Spencer. This time I'll let him get caught while John and I make our escape.

George stands for a moment to see, then ducks back down behind the wall.

"Who is that?" he asks, but I don't answer. I peek over the top, watch as the man circles the back of the house. He pulls at the windows, but they're locked tight.

"Liza," George says urgently. His face has gone white.

There's a howling of wind and a crowd of shadowy figures walk out from the trees and float down the valley. They circle the stone wall and surround the house. The rain curves around them, making their shapes clearer to see, their strands of white hair blowing behind them.

"You see them too?"

His face gives all the answer I need. He presses his back against the stone and holds his flashlight against his chest as if it will protect him.

The detective doesn't seem to notice the shadows. He keeps looking for a way inside, a way to search my things, discover my secret, declare us frauds and lock us up forever. He hasn't yet tried the door, doesn't suspect that it might be open—the beam is still lifted from when I ran outside.

"Wait here," I say. "Shine your light at them if they get close."

All George can do is nod. He's shaking, and not from the cold, even though the rain is near freezing and has plastered his hair to his forehead.

I curl my fingers over the stone wall, push off from the ground, and leap to the other side.

The detective is distracted. He'll never see me as long as I'm careful. I have to get closer. I have to know who he is.

The shadows are drawn to the house, moving closer. The rain pours harder, spouting like fountains off the corners of the roof.

Another bolt of lightning comes, and I see the man clearly for a moment, the image baking into my eyes.

It's that old, hunched-over man with the white hair and fogged glasses, except now the powder has washed from his hair, revealing thick black strands. His glasses are different, too, and he stands up straight, moving with the speed of a much younger man.

I gasp, and gooseflesh sprouts on my arms. I try to think back to everything that old man has seen. Have I talked to John around him? What does he know?

There's a scream from behind me. George is surrounded by shadows, and the rain that's near him is a distorted thing, falling around the figures' shoulders, a crowd of transparent bodies with glowing white eyes.

The flashlight blinks on and off, on and off, and George spins in place.

One grips his arm, pulling him closer, and the flashlight beam burst into its face. Another wraps its arm around George's chest and he squirms and tries to aim, but the metal handle is wet and slippery and falls to the ground. I run to him.

"Get off him! He's not who you want!"

The storm rages on above us, circling, like it's a monster waiting to strike.

"Hey! You there!" the man shouts from behind me. He's heard our screams, and he's running toward us, but I don't even care anymore. I need to save my friend.

Leaping over the wall, I push through the shadows, grab the flashlight from the ground and aim it—

flash flash flash flash

—so that it cascades the figures in light. They break apart into little pieces, and the rain carries them away.

For a moment, I think the button has stuck, because a tear of light rips through the sky, revealing a field of yellow, a perfect day, just like in my memories before the sickness came. The light grows, the hole between worlds opens wider, and the smells change—honeysuckle and grass, all the sweetness of spring air.

I can see the other side. I crawl toward it, and the shadows come behind me, seem to push me closer.

My body fights against me, and my head spins. I don't want to faint, not now, not when the detective is so close.

The light is right in front of me. I fall forward, and my fingers curl into the mud. I try to push myself up, but can't. All I can do is reach out my hand, try to touch it, feel its warmth, and if I could only—

"I just need to talk to you," the detective says. He steps in front of me, close to the light, his foot grazing the edge.

"Stay back," I try to say, but I'm not sure if the words have actually formed. It's too late. The light grows and he steps into it, falling through the tear, wrapped into the world of golden rays. The edges close around him, and in a burst, he's gone.

The world is dark again, and the rain hammers the ground.

"George!" I call out, looking up at the sky, seeing the clouds bubbling above, watching their strange colors.

"I'm here," he says, spinning in place, looking for more shadows. For now, they seem to have moved on.

"You need to go home," I say.

He's breathing hard, and his body shakes. His eyes dart around the yard, over the house, up the valley.

"Listen to me, George. It's not safe for you here."

I grab his face in my hands and make him focus on me.

"Go. I'll see you again. I promise."

I place the flashlight in his hands, and he nods.

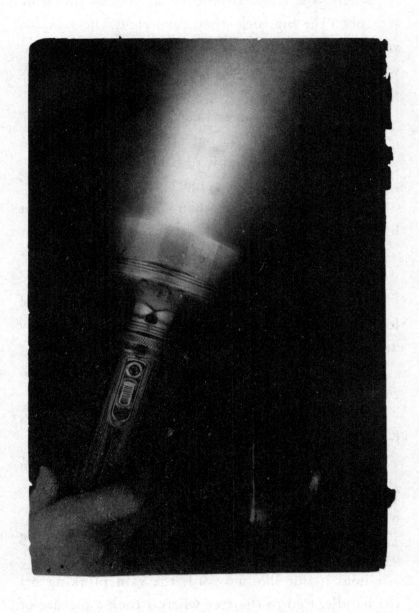

"When you come to the barn, follow the wide stream to the big rock, then turn right," he says, his voice shaking. "Take the narrow path. It's the fastest way through the woods. I'll come find you when the storm passes."

"I'll be there as soon as I can. I promise."

He holds his flashlight out to me.

"Take this. You'll need it to find your way."

"But how will you get home?"

"I know the way better than you do. I can make it in the dark."

"Are you sure?"

"It's a gift."

I hug him tightly, then pull the folded picture of John and me with the ghost of Mrs. Turner from my dress.

"And here's my gift to you. If I don't make it, you can remember me with it," I say. "Now go."

The shadows will be back, and the farther he gets from this house, the safer he'll be.

He runs up the hill and into the woods. I'm alone again, and the storm continues, unstoppable, gathering strength.

I clutch the flashlight and circle the house, heading back to my basement window.

I hold it out like a sword, the rain plinking off the handle. I go to the tree where I took a picture of

Charles. Three shadows circle it, and I aim the light at them and—

Flash.

The beam cuts through them, shining off the tree. They burst apart like pieces of ash floating from a fire and drift away. I spin. The shadows have re-formed behind me, eyes glowing white, and—

Flash.

More of them move around the stone wall, around the porch. Everywhere.

What have I brought to this place?

What will happen to the others inside the Society if we don't get away?

I never wanted anyone to get hurt.

Shadows circle the outhouses and the little cemetery. I aim the light at them—*flash flash flash*—breaking them apart for brief moments.

I'm coming for you, John, I think. *As soon as I see you, we're leaving.*

In the morning, Mr. Spencer and the guests will be distracted by the storm. We just need to find the right moment to run.

I sneak into the basement and hide in my room, tucking my head under the blankets.

I wait, maybe I sleep, and a few hours later I hear footsteps above, dull thunking over the rain. The smell of the cooks preparing breakfast wafts through the floorboards.

I change out of my wet clothes and slip on dark pants and a shirt that I stole from a boy at the house we stayed at a few stops ago, in a town I hardly remember.

Perfect for a runaway.

Today is the day.

I pull the suitcase from under the bed and place the flashlight inside, check that everything is packed in my Hidden Place, then lay the false bottom in place and close the lid. I move it by the door so it's ready for me, then wait until I hear the heavy clunking of Charles's boots on the stairs.

"Liza," Charles says, tapping on my door and cracking it open. He raises his eyebrows at my outfit but doesn't say a word about it. "Everything all right?"

"Yes, sir."

"Come with me. We must be careful. I don't think we've seen the worst of this yet."

He's right. I can feel it. There's no time to waste. The storms won't stop until I go, and I have to save this place from more damage.

He leads me through the basement, past the tripod standing underneath a long string of pictures nailed to the rafters, each trembling with their ghosts.

PART THREE

THE
STORM

THE FAMILY

This morning is dark as the night, and the wind is blowing so hard that the trees outside groan and bend. Every so often, a limb snaps and falls to the ground. Inside, pictures wobble on the walls. The whole house seems to shiver.

The storm is at the front of everyone's mind, and there isn't much talk about the missing man, just bits of gossip.

"He must have left before the storm hit," a man says.

"I heard his things were still in his room."

"Lord, help him if he's out in this."

Fox paces the entryway, whining and scratching at the walls. John calls to her and she sits beside him, panting heavily.

I sneak behind him and whisper, "Stay close to me today. We're going to run."

He tilts his head at me, then looks back out the window.

"Don't talk nonsense, Liza. Look at that storm."

He's right, of course. It's foolish to consider, but no rain or wind will stop me from getting away from the shadows.

"It will stop once we leave."

John glances into the parlor where a small crowd is gathering at the window, watching the wind rip planks from the house and lightning explode in the sky.

"What do you think happened to the man?"

I hoped he wouldn't ask me this, because the truth sounds far-fetched. But maybe he needs to hear it.

"He went to the other side. I tried to stop him. It was an accident, John. If we stay in this place any longer, everyone's in danger."

"Why do you think we caused this?" he asks, but we're interrupted by an explosion as a board flies through the window and shatters it to pieces, pushing the crowd back into the hallway. They close the doors to the parlor, and through the glass panels I watch as a table and chairs are blown to the side.

Fox barks and cries.

"Everyone back! Away from the windows!" Charles commands.

"Don't panic," Ms. Eldridge says. "This place has survived worse, I'm certain, and can handle a little storm."

"Get whatever you need," I tell John, searching the crowd for Mr. Spencer. He's far in the back, not watching. "When no one's looking, we're leaving."

"All activities are cancelled until further notice, and we ask that you stay inside," Charles announces.

There's grumbling in the crowd, but Ms. Eldridge adds, "We simply can't risk sending anyone to the other side by accident, can we?"

It's a joke, I think, but no one laughs.

Charles points out the window.

"Were we expecting new guests?"

Ms. Eldridge glides beside him and squints at the field. Coming through the trees and down the lane is a horse and carriage. The horse pulls against the wind, its face battered and blown.

"No, we certainly were not," Ms. Eldridge says, grabbing Charles's hand. "I'll get towels. Wave them in."

Lightning roars above them, a chill goes down my spine—on the far side of the field, shadows appear, watching the house.

Fox paws at my legs and I rub her ears.

"It's all right, girl. You'll be all right."

"Who could they be?" a man asks.

"Passing travelers, caught in the storm," Charles says. "We should let them stay, only until it passes."

"Are they any safer here?" a woman asks, looking

into the parlor where rain and leaves are swirling into the room.

Charles runs into the rain and waves at the cab, and the driver directs the horse toward the gate. The creature's feet stick in the mud and it struggles with each step to pull them free.

"Poor souls," a woman mutters.

Charles directs them to the front of the house and a family leaps from the cab and runs inside, covering their heads with their hands as if that will help at all. The shadows are all around the wall now, and the rain beads off their bodies, making them plain to see. Everyone's distracted by the dark clouds twirling above. They look like an ocean in revolt, and strange colors dance along the surface.

The mother enters first, followed by a boy and girl—both no older than John—and the father hauls a case in with the driver. They stand in the entranceway, soaking wet and shivering.

The father rubs his hands over his thinning hair and says, "We were heading toward Maryland. We'd hoped to arrive at my brother's house before dinner . . . but . . . the winds . . . and the rain . . . Lord, help us . . ."

"It's another freak storm," Charles says.

"Yes," the father says. "The sky was clear when we left, but then the clouds moved in so quickly and—"

The father studies the room, realizes for the first time that this isn't a normal house or hotel. A question forms on his lips, but he doesn't ask it. "Thank you all for taking us in."

Ms. Eldridge returns with towels and drapes them over their shoulders, and the son and daughter step forward to look over the faces in the crowd.

"Where are we?" the boy asks, and the father laughs uncomfortably and pulls him close.

"Don't be rude, son. My name is Robert Scott," he says. "This is my wife, Mary, and my children, William and Heidi."

The girl looks at me and smiles, and I feel like I'm looking at myself from the before times, when I was part of a family, too.

Memories are coming back, but I push them down. *Not now.*

"We're pleased to have you," Ms. Eldridge says, not bothering to tell them any more about where they are.

"Are you hungry? There's plenty in the kitchen."

"No," the father says. "We're fine."

Another sound comes from outside, close and big. The big oak tree cracks in the middle and falls, crashing into the wall and toppling the stones. The electricity to the house cuts out, and the little oil lamps are the only light left. The guests gasp and huddle closer.

"We should go down to the basement," Charles says, and Ms. Eldridge nods, leading a line of people down.

I move closer to John and we look out the window at the broken tree. Heavy currents of rain pummel the ground and blot the windows. It comes in waves. The shadows are circling the yard now, their bodies slanted against the wind. I try to ignore them.

The young boy, William, moves toward John and Fox and pats the little dog's head. She whines and paces in a circle.

The crowd of guests moves around me, and Charles takes my hand. I get caught in the flow, pushed toward the basement stairs.

John's frozen in place, staring outside at the storm, at those shapes moving with the rain.

I want to call out to him, tell him to follow me down, but Mr. Spencer is nearby, and I can't have him watching me closely today. I'm pulled downstairs and Fox follows beside me, leaning her shaking body against my legs.

"Sit against the walls," Ms. Eldridge commands. "Far away from the windows."

More oil lamps are lit and they flicker against the walls. The rain is muffled down here.

I move toward the family and sit beside William and Heidi. Their clothes are still sopping wet under the towels, and a small bead of water comes from Heidi's leg and hits the floor, *drip drip drip*, like a bit of the storm has snuck into the basement.

There are things that only children can see, Ms. Eldridge told me. Will they see the shadows too? Are they safe here?

Heidi looks at me and smiles.

"Hello," she says, and Mr. Spencer hovers in the corner, tapping his foot, letting me know he's listening. "Do you live here?"

"No."

"Of course, she doesn't," William tells his sister. "It's a hotel."

"It's not a hotel," their father says. "Now stop talking."

"This is a special place, dear, close to the other side," a woman says.

"Please. I'll have none of this witchcraft around my children."

Their father stands and looks out the little window to the cemetery, judging which is more dangerous, to stay in this place or go back into the storm. The wind and rain convinces him to sit.

Here in the dark basement, the flickering light and shadows from the lamps make it hard to see anything clearly. I scan the room for John, but can't find him among the faces.

"Who'd like their photo taken?" Mr. Spencer asks,

his voice slurring as he hits his knuckles on the chest containing Charles's camera equipment. He pulls out the camera and a flash.

"Now is *not* the time," Ms. Eldridge says, and Mr. Spencer waves her off.

"Oh, why not?" He waves his arms in a wide motion. "Let's have a little fun. The spirits are *here* today. Can you feel them?"

I'm not listening to him. Panic grips my chest as I scan the room, still looking for John. I shouldn't have come down here without him.

"I'd like mine taken," a woman says, and others join in. A line forms behind Mr. Spencer.

In the corner of my eyes I see the shadows floating along the walls. Heidi stares at them and grabs her brother's hand.

I touch her arm, whisper, "Don't look at them. They don't want you."

They want John.

I stand, hoping the line of guests behind Mr. Spencer will distract the others, and slink along the edge of the basement, working my way to the stairs. There's nothing blocking me from them now, so I wait for the perfect moment.

Soon, Mr. Spencer leans over the camera in the middle of the room, framing a photograph of a woman on the stool. He tells her to sit straight, hold her chin up, and when the shutter clicks and the flash ignites, I run up the stairs, taking them three at a time. Fox barks, and I feel every eye in the basement turn to me.

Charles yells out, "Where are you going? Someone stop her!" but I'm too fast. I open the door to the upstairs just as another gust of wind shakes the house.

"John!" I scream.

The front door to the house rattles and bursts open, torn from its hinges. Water pours in, soaking the front mat. The house brightens with a green glow and the pots in the kitchen shake.

"I'm upstairs," he yells, but it's faint.

Why did you go up there? I think, and as if he can read my thoughts, he says, "I'm hiding, Liza. The shadows want to take me."

I move to the stairs, wrap my hand around the bannister, and climb to the upper level.

The hallway is narrower than I remember from that first night, and the floorboards creak under my feet.

It's so dark without a single lamp on. I wish I had George's flashlight with me. I run my hands along the wall, feeling for one of the little tables that line the hallway. My hand bumps against one. I steady a wobbling lamp and open the drawer, feeling for a box of matches. I grab it and light the lamp, but the glow is so faint in the hall that it barely makes a difference. I take the matches with me and light another one, holding it in front of my eyes, turning the corner toward Mr. Spencer's room. John's room must be near his, though I've never seen where he and Mr. Spencer sleep.

"John!"

Some of the doors to the other rooms are open and the rain pounds against the windows. I feel like I'm on a great ship, rocking back and forth on the waves, and the whole thing could tip over at any moment and sink down into the sea.

The match burns out and I drop its remains on the floor. A dark shadow moves across the hall. It's the form of a man. I can see a face and shoulders, paper thin, but his body blurs and fades by the midsection.

I fall back, light another match, throw it, and the shape fades away, re-forming somewhere else.

"Help me, Liza!"

"I'm coming!"

Pulling myself up, I light another match and hold the little flame in front of me, continuing on, looking over my shoulder for more.

Mr. Spencer's door is at the end of the hall. It's cracked open, and I can see dirty clothes draped over the headboard, a row of empty glass bottles stacked in neat little rows on the dresser. The bed is unmade, with a dark outline of sweat on the sheets. The smell is strong and sour. John is there, tucked in a corner, shaking.

"I've seen the shadows since we came here, Liza," he says. "I only pretended I didn't."

I *knew* he did, but why would he lie?

Grabbing his shoulders, I pull him close, stare into his eyes.

"Why would you do that? I thought I was losing my mind."

"Because I was scared. They're trying to take me with them. I thought if we ignored them, they'd—"

"You don't need to be scared. I won't let them. You're going to get better. That's why we need to leave. I know a place where we can stay."

He looks at me but doesn't say anything.

"How long can we run, Liza?"

As long as we have to.

The match burns out and the rain hits the window so hard that I wonder if this ship has already sunk and we're heading deep underwater. How could I tell? Waves pass over the glass, and I stand beside John to look out the window and see the shadows move across the yard, getting closer and closer.

"Go without me," he says. "I'll just slow you down."

"Never."

I think of George with his family, probably tucked safely in the basement of their house, waiting for this storm to pass. We can make it to the barn, I know we can. We'll never stop running.

Down the hall, a window breaks, and I hear a stream of water pouring inside.

"Don't leave my side," I say, pulling John from the bed.

I light another match and ease my head out into the hall, look left then right. It's too dark to see anything, but if we close our eyes and run, we can—

A shadow of a woman moves in front of us.

"Who are you?" I call out, but she doesn't answer.

She comes toward us, reaching out a hand. It passes through me and clutches John's shoulder, pulling him toward the window.

"Let him go!" I scream, throwing the match at her. The little light doesn't get close enough to make a difference. It falls to the floor and fizzles against the hardwood.

I light another match, wave it around her, and for a moment her face is bright. Her milky white eyes stare into mine before they break into pieces. Her body seems to float away, down into the floor.

I light another match and pull John into the

hallway, not bothering to look first. We press on, turning the corner and moving toward the stairs. The house rumbles. A picture falls in the hallway, and the frame shatters. Shards of glass spread around my feet.

When we pass the door to Charles's room, I step inside and look out the window. There are more shadows than I can count, coming from the woods, filling the valley, climbing over the stone wall. Light carves the sky like a knife, ripping through the thin place.

Liza!

Two shapes appear behind us, rising from the floor. They grab John's arms and lift him up. His feet lift from the floor, and they pull toward the hall.

"No!"

I light another match and throw it. Then another and another, before grabbing his ankle and pulling him back to me.

"Stop it!"

John falls to the floor, coughing hard.

There are only seven matches left in the box, and there's so many shadows.

"Can you make it downstairs?"

"Just . . . just give me some . . . time . . . to catch my . . . breath," he says, coughing again.

Stay with me.

I slide my arms under John's to carry him. Despite how thin he is, he's surprisingly heavy, and I take the stairs slowly until we're at the bottom. My arms ache. I'll never be able to carry him all the way to George's house. *No.* I can't think like that. I'll do it. I have to. Otherwise this whole house and everyone in it is in danger of being pulled to the other side like that pile of stones and the detective.

Through the broken front door, I can see the tear of light, its edges crackling with energy. A silhouette of a man appears in the center of the light, staggering, pushing his way through. I know his walk now, can see the distinctive glasses on his face.

The detective.

He holds out a hand, pushes through. For a moment, it seems like the light has exploded and he passes through the thin place and collapses into the wet mud.

The sky is ripping apart, so bright that I can't see shadows around it but I know they are near. I've seen them, and it won't be long until more find their way in.

The detective crawls on his hands and knees until he reaches the porch's railing, then pulls himself up. He staggers inside and sees me. John wraps his arms around my waist, using me like a shield.

"You," he says, gasping. Rain pours down his brow. "What did you do to me?"

I don't answer.

He rubs his head, feeling for a wound.

"You hit me."

"No," I say. He doesn't seem to remember where he was. Or maybe he can't. Maybe it's too much to accept.

He pushes past me to the basement door and rips it open, calls for help, and the crowd of people below answer him.

More shadows appear at the door, as if taunting me, daring me to go out into the storm. Seven matches. That's all I have.

I need something brighter. The flashlight is back in my Hidden Place, down in the basement with everything else I own.

I curse myself for not bringing it up with me.

I have to act fast.

Racking my brain for a solution, a plan forms. I can hide John, just long enough to sneak down and get it. The shadows fade in the light, and it's the only way we can get to George's barn. The tear will heal without us here, and then Charles, Margaret, Ms. Eldridge, and all the other guests will be saved.

I pull John into one of the hidden corridors tucked

behind the kitchen. Water drips between the slatted boards, and the ceiling is soft and damp.

"I have to leave you here for a moment," I tell John, and I get on my knees to look him in the eyes. "I need to get something—I promise I'll be right back." I place the box of matches beside him. "Take this. There's only a few left, but if the shadows come, light one. Don't let them get you."

He doesn't answer.

"John, do you understand me?"

His eyes dart between me and the door. The streak of light is growing, expanding, coming toward us. I can feel the harsh glow from the light outside hit the side of my face.

"Is this really what you want?" he asks as he glances into the light. The glow illuminates his tears.

"What do you mean?"

"Running away. Living like this forever."

"Of course, it's what I want. Isn't it what you want?"

Why does he have to ask silly questions? Why now?

"I just want to know you'll be all right when I'm gone," he says, and I pull him close, wrap him in my arms.

"Don't ever talk like that, John," I say. "We'll never be apart. Can you use the matches?"

He nods and places his hand on top of them.

"I'll be quick," I say, then run through the hall, eyes closed to block out the shadows, and race down the basement steps, praying I won't be seen and that John will still be there when I return.

A FRAUD EXPOSED

The basement is humid, packed with bodies, and it rumbles with excitement. Something is happening. Screams and shouts drown out the wind and rain, and as soon as I appear, all eyes turn to me.

"There she is! Someone grab her!" the detective yells.

People turn to me, unsure of what I've done, but ready to move.

"She's an evil thing," he growls, an angry fire burning in his eyes. "She's a fraud, and she's working with him!"

He points at Mr. Spencer.

"I can prove it."

He opens the door to my room, grabs my suitcase, opens the latch, and shakes it. My clothes fall out, and then the hidden compartment opens, spilling the rest of my secrets on the floor. There's a stack of uncut pictures, cotton balls, and the black-painted board. My camera smacks against the ground, and the wooden frame cracks. The flashlight hits the ground and rolls across the basement floor, through a maze of legs.

"There! You see?"

The stool and tripod in the center of the room topple as a group of men grab Mr. Spencer by his arms and hold him tight.

Outside, the shadows move with the rain, the tear of light pulsing and growing, heading toward the house.

Mr. Spencer thrashes his arms, breaking free of the men.

"Get them both!" someone yells, and more people surround him.

I turn to run, but Charles has worked his way to the stairs and takes them in long strides, his arm wrapping around my shoulder and holding on tight. He pulls me down to the basement floor.

"It'll be all right," he whispers to me, but I kick my legs and thrash, trying to escape his hold.

"What's the meaning of all this?" Ms. Eldridge asks.

"I've been following Spencer for months," the detective says. "And that girl has been with him the whole time, traveling from city to city, helping him with his lie."

"That's impossible!" a woman says, and all eyes turn to me. The crowd closes in.

"These people are crafty," the detective continues. "Ask yourself, when did the girl arrive?"

A guest who has been here since the start nods his head and yells, "She came the very same night! We thought she was a runaway."

"You see?" the man asks. "It was all an orchestrated con, right from the very beginning. Who are they, really?"

"I could ask you the same. Who are *you*, sir?" Charles asks, his arm still wrapped around me, and I can't tell if it's to restrain or protect me.

"My name is Simon Hall, and I am with the American Society for Psychical Research, headquartered in New York City." He pulls out a piece of paper and waves it around the room. "One of our duties to the Spiritualist community is exposing *frauds* like these, though I should think by now we wouldn't have to expose something so ridiculous as spirits in photographs. When this storm is over, I'd like to turn them over to authorities in New York so they can be held accountable for their disgraceful crimes and thefts."

All this time I thought he was a detective with the police, but this is even worse. Even stepping over to the other side hasn't changed his mind. If anything it's made his beliefs stronger.

Charles looks at me. I expected him to be

disappointed, but there's no emotion on his face. It's as blank as the day he drove Madam Crimson away.

"I'm so sorry. I didn't have a choice," I whisper. "But you have to let me go. John is up there. He's really my brother, and they're trying to get us. If the thin place tears—"

Charles looks at me, bewildered, and then asks, "Who?"

"The shadows," I say.

The basement goes deathly silent except for the pouring rain. Everyone looks at Mr. Spencer and then me, back and forth, waiting for one of us to move.

Charles's grip loosens right as the chanting starts. One person begins, and then the whole room falls into that familiar rhythm of *fraud, fraud, fraud*. Along the edges of the room I see shapes move, surrounding us, pushing us closer. Fox howls at the ceiling, and the wind roars outside.

"Stop!" Ms. Eldridge says. "Everyone settle down!"

Only the family that was caught in the rain doesn't join in. They watch the whole scene from their spot near the stairs, unsure of what they're seeing, and I try to work my way toward them, bumping against bodies, shaking free of grasping hands, forcing myself through.

Fraud! Fraud! Fraud!

Behind me, Mr. Spencer screams out, fighting his way through.

"Please!" Ms. Eldridge yells. "There is more to it than this! I knew they were together from the start."

The chants continue, the crowd tightens around us.

"I've seen all the con man tricks, and there's nothing new about having your helper arrive later. You must stop before—"

But the crowd is too far gone. No one listens to her, and their chant drowns her out.

She knew? Is that why she paid for the supplies and let me guard the photographic plates? All this time, I thought I was so clever. Another thought occurs to me—did Charles know, too? I thought he really wanted me to be his assistant, but he was just keeping a close eye on me.

I can't get to my suitcase now. My Hidden Place is ruined, everything is out now.

I search the floor for the flashlight, but all I see are legs and feet, caught in a blur of motion.

"Don't let her escape!" a man yells as I push closer to the stairs.

Heidi and William are the only things in front of me, blocking my path.

"I need your help!" I yell over the chanting, and they watch the shadows on the walls, surrounding the chanting guests. "I know you see them too. I need to save my brother!"

"Your brother?" William asks.

"Please," I whisper. "I have to get him."

Heidi nods and raises her arm from behind her back, revealing my flashlight. She must have grabbed it off the floor when it flew from my suitcase. The side is scraped and the glass disc in front of the bulb is cracked, but when I take it and push the button—*flash*—it still works.

"Thank you," I say, and the children step aside. I run up the stairs, falling to my hands and knees and pulling myself up and out of the basement.

"Liza! Wait!" Mr. Spencer screams, but I don't look back. I should have never come down here.

Fraud! Fraud! Fraud! comes from all around me.

"John!" I yell.

Behind me, I hear Ms. Eldridge announce, "Let them go," but it doesn't matter now because I'm at the top, and I run down the hall and open the door to the little corridor. The box of matches are still there, the paper soaked through, lying in a puddle of water. John is gone.

"Where are you?"

There's no answer.

I hit the button of the flashlight, but farther in, the corridor is empty, so I run back into the hall, *flash flash flash*, painting circles of light on the walls.

With a crash, Mr. Spencer bursts from the basement. His clothes are torn and his hands and face are scraped. He looks at me and sneers, moves toward me, and—

flash

—he squints at my light and covers his eyes, then turns and runs through the broken front door and out into the yard. The rain and wind hit him with such a force that he falls to his side, bracing himself against the storm. He runs toward the gate in the stone wall, passing through a crowd of shadowy figures, pushing through them like they're not even there. I move to the door. The rain has soaked the front entrance and blown the curtains from the windows. Clouds swirl around us, and if you look out, it seems like the house is spinning in place.

"Liza!"

I turn and see John in the parlor. Shapes surround him, coming through the windows, out of the hidden corridors, from the kitchen and the stairs. They're everywhere, filling the house.

They reach out, grab his arms and legs, drag him toward the window in the direction of the growing tear of light.

I run to him, hit the flashlight's button again and again, aiming its beam at each of their faces.

Flash flash flash flash.

Their white eyes stare at me and they release their grip, fade back into the floor, and John collapses. His small body shakes, and I aim the flashlight around the room, pointing it at any shadow I see, on and off, on and off, until the room is empty, and the metal handle gets hot to the touch.

I cradle John in my arms, wipe the hair from his eyes.

"We ain't gonna make it," he whispers.

"We *are* going to make it," I say, but I'm not even sure I believe that. "I promise you that we will. They won't take you."

I pull him to his feet, lead him back to the front door. I hold out the flashlight and aim it, hit the button with my thumb and watch as it illuminates the hallway.

Empty.

Outside, a large form moves in front of the door, and I aim the flashlight at its eyes and hit the button.

Flash.

It explodes into a dark mist, sinking into the ground, snaking backward, little slivers of shadow that form again with the others in the yard. The tear is widening, and through it, I can see a summer day. More shadows pour from the circle of light. Will the shadows follow us to George's barn? Will the thin place heal as soon as we're gone?

"Close your eyes, John. Walk with me."

I wrap my arm around him and keep the flashlight trained in front of us, heading out into the storm.

INTO THE STORM

The wind is worse than the rain, an invisible force that pushes against us. In a moment, we're drenched and cold. Our hair sticks to our foreheads, and our clothes cling heavily to our bodies.

Water pours over the side of the flashlight, and I smack the side and hit the button. *Nothing.* I try to protect it against the rain, tucking it under my shirt so only the small circular glass lens is visible, and hit the button again.

Flash.

It flickers, just a small glow out in the darkness, but thank goodness it still works. In the yard, there are so many shadows, surrounding the broken tree, moving around the cemetery stones, and filling the courtyard. They stand rigid against the gusting wind, and through the sheets of rain I can see their thin bodies and blurred faces, their dim white eyes, their cotton-colored hair. Long arms wave at me like dark ribbons, their fingers slithering toward us. I flash the light directly at one and it explodes into bits of shadow and gets pulled back into the glow.

The light continues to grow, spinning, crackling, ripping its way through the barrier between our worlds. It inches closer to the house, the edge of its glow touching the steps that lead to the front porch. The wood disappears.

I think of all those people in the basement, and what would happen to them if the tear would rip open wide and take them all.

The family that just arrived is there too. With their two children, they remind me of my own family, years ago. If nothing else, I have to save them.

I think of what Charles told me that first day at breakfast, pointing at the part where the blade met the handle.

This house sits on a spot where the wall is exceptionally thin. Do you understand what that means?

It means I can't be here a moment longer. It means I need to find a place where the barrier is thick, where no one knows us and no one believes.

"Get away from us!" I scream at the shadows, pulling John along and hitting the button again and again. The beam from my flashlight is small, eaten up by all the darkness.

The shadows surround us, blocking the path to the front gate.

"Let us leave!"

Flash flash flash.

It doesn't do much. They're not close enough yet. Two step forward, heading toward us, their eyes glowing from a light reflected from far away.

"You can't take him from me," I say, and the storm seems to answer. Lightning rips across the sky. Wind roars and a gust blows down the hill. It passes through the shadows but knocks John and me to the ground.

They reach out and grab us. Their hands feel like a cold breath wrapping around my skin. They pull us to our feet and turn to John.

"I'm sorry," John says. "You can't fight them all."

I can.

He holds out his arms, no longer fighting, and the two shadows take him and pull him along the grass. His feet slide against the wet earth, and the crowd of shadows follow.

"Stop!"

I run after them, fumbling with my flashlight. The shadows are fast, and I need to be close if there's any chance of the beam working.

I aim—*flash flash*—and the beam breaks some of them apart, sending them back to the light. They release their grasp on John, and I wrap an arm around him and keep the flashlight out with my other hand, even though the rain pounds against the metal tube and enters the cracks. I drag him across the yard, working our way to the gate.

Up the hill, I can see Mr. Spencer running on the road toward the woods. He's struggling in the mud and against the wind.

"Help us!" I yell, but I'm not sure if he can hear me.

The shadows follow us. They grab at John's arms, trying to pull him from my grasp, trying to take him from me.

Flash flash flash.

The light from the bulb is getting weaker, and the lens is covered in beads of water.

Flash flash.

My arm aches. I can't hold on.

He slides from my arms and collapses into the ground. The shadows reach out for him, but I'm ready for them now. I pull out the flashlight, move close and hit the button, again and again, shining it into their milky eyes.

"Go away!"

Flash.

A shadow wraps its arms around John's chest, lifting him to his feet.

I hit the button again.

Flash.

The flashlight blinks and flickers. The beam is dying, and when I shake it, water pours from the front.

The shadow pulls him higher, up into the air, and it looks like he's floating now.

"Leave him!"

I push the button over and over, as hard as I can, and a tiny bit of light comes out—*flash*—just enough that the shadow releases him and retreats, watching from a distance, waiting for another moment to grab. I hold John tight, wiping the water from his eyes.

"Stay with me," I whisper, and then look out at the crowd of shadows, dozens of their white eyes focused on us.

The rain slides around them, and they seem almost as solid as the people inside the house now. I should have left this place the first chance I had. I saw them that first night in the back room with the bath. Tried to convince myself I didn't, but deep down, I knew what I saw. I could have taken John and run. Why didn't I?

More shadows float down the hill and flow into the yard, coming through the stone wall where the fallen tree has left a giant hole littered with rocks and mortar.

I struggle to pull John through the front courtyard.

He's so heavy and the wind pushes us back. My feet slide on the wet stones.

Looking back, I see that the light has stopped its slow crawl toward the house. It's changed course, coming toward us.

We can keep running. We can always stay ahead of it.

"Help!" I yell again, hoping Mr. Spencer will hear us. He's gone off the road, struggling up the hill that leads through the tunnel of trees.

We have to catch him.

"Wait for us!" I scream, louder than I've ever screamed before. Mr. Spencer throws back his head, and a growl of laughter cuts through the rain.

"They're trying to take him from me!"

He doesn't come to help. He claws up the hill and disappears into the trees. I'll have to save John on my own.

We move through the gate and out onto the muddy road. Small rivers run along the sides, cutting deep trenches into the earth. Big black clouds boil overhead, and when another gust of wind blows, there are cracking sounds in the woods as trees are ripped in half.

We keep moving, keep pushing. I limp along, dragging John with me. My fingernails dig into his ribs. The road has turned into a thick soup of mud and stones, and I fall to my knees and slide down, dropping the flashlight. It sticks into the ground with a slurp.

I pull it out and hit the button, but the water has seeped the whole way through and when I hit the button—*click*—nothing happens. I throw it into the field and start to cry.

"We can't run from them forever," John says.

The shadows are following, marching behind us. There's too many of them to count, and they move against the rain, their feet never touching the ground.

The light is coming with us. It's passed over the wall now, devouring the stones in its path. It tears through the ground, leaving a trail of golden-lit grass behind it. It tears deeper into the thin place, and I can see the summer meadow through it, just for an instant, so bright it sends sparks in my vision.

Why is it still following us? How far away from this place do we have to be?

I pull John into the grass.

"Can you walk?"

"No, Liza."

I drag him up the hill, fighting against the weight of his body.

I pull John into the woods. The trees greet us like tall, silent guardians, protecting us from the storm. Some rain gets through their branches but it's softer now. The wind stills howls around us, whistling as it rushes through the messy tangle of branches.

I can see Mr. Spencer ahead. He drags himself over twisted plants and fallen trees and stares back at us.

"I don't want you!" he screams. "Stay away!"

I point at the light and the shadows behind us sparkling in the rain and the eerie glow.

"We need your help! They're trying to take him!"

The shadows wait on the hill, watching us, and now I can see their faces even clearer, the outline of their shoulders, the curve of their cheeks. They're people of all different shapes and sizes, coming into focus.

I pull John up on top of a pile of rocks, but they're wet and slippery and we slide across the ground, traveling worn pathways through the trees. I search for anything familiar. It's been dark the last few times I've been in the woods, so I try to remember that first time I traveled through them. I think I've been here before. I think this is the way.

There's a rushing sound nearby, and the stream that cuts through the woods is up ahead. Today, it's overflowing and raging, too wide to jump over and too fast to walk through.

Follow the wide stream to the big rock, then turn right, George said. *Take the narrow path.*

"I know where we can go!" I yell. "Wait for us!"

"There is no *us*," Mr. Spencer replies. "There's only *you*."

I wanted to get away from him, but now I'll take any help I can get.

"Stop! You're going to die out here! I know a place that's safe."

He's turned around, coming at me through the trees.

"Run, Liza," John says, or is that the voice in my head?

Only a faint shape of him can be seen through the branches. Leaves and limbs rustle around us.

Run!

I look down at John, long enough to take my attention away from Mr. Spencer, who then bursts through the branches and grabs my wrist, his eyes wild and dark.

"Where can we go?" he yells over the rain.

"It's a barn. A few miles away."

"How can I trust anything from you? You've told nothing but lies since the day you came," he hisses, pulling my face close to his.

"Let go of me!"

"I've never known if you really believed what you say, or if this was some game to you."

John's too heavy to hold. I let him go and he falls to the ground.

"John!"

"I think I know the answer now," he says. "Do you need me to say it again?"

I try to pull free, try to cover my ears with my hands but his grip is too tight.

Don't listen to him.

"I've told you the truth so many times and you never seem to remember. It's almost like you *can't.*"

"Don't," I beg, looking behind me. "Don't say it again. Not in front of him."

The shadows are moving in the trees now, but there's still an opening toward the stream. If I get free I can—

"John's dead, Liza. He was gone before you ever came to me."

THE CLEARING

The lies we tell ourselves are the strongest kind.

I haven't been telling myself the truth, have I?

I look down at John. Rain streaks down his face and I rub my hand along his cheek. The tear of light is getting closer to us, moving through the trees. We need to keep moving.

"Don't listen, John. He's a liar. That's all he is."

"Liza, tell me you understand," Mr. Spencer says.

How many times has he told me this? I can't remember. I always try not to listen, try not to let the words take root in my mind.

"It's not true," I say. I leap at him and grab his coat, hit his chest with my hands, but he shakes me off.

I think of all the stops we've been to, all the dark bedrooms and closets I've worked in, preparing paper ghosts to fool the living. I hid him in the shadows, kept him out of sight, to protect him. Didn't I?

He was gone before you ever came to me.

Mr. Spencer's words ring in my mind.

It's been different here at the Society. I've had to let John out in the open, amongst the other guests. Have I ever seen anyone talk to him since we arrived?

"Liza, stop thinking," John says.

No, it can't be true. Fox followed him everywhere, nuzzling her head against his legs.

Dogs are very sensitive to spirits, Ms. Eldridge once said. And have I ever seen her talk to John? Maybe. Or was she talking to Fox?

John seems to be fading before my eyes, the colors inverting. He's turning into one of them, a negative image of himself. A shadow person.

Stop thinking.

Gooseflesh rises on my arms and neck.

"Do you know what I was burying that night in the woods?" Mr. Spencer asks. "After that little scene in the assembly hall, I needed to hide any evidence of our relation. Death notices. Paperwork. Things that told the truth about us. About your family. Do we need to dredge this up again?"

I shake my head. "You're lying!"

"Follow me."

I need to stop him. I don't want to look at anything.

"Maybe this will prove it to you once and for all."

Mr. Spencer turns and runs across a small tree trunk that has fallen over the raging stream.

"No," I growl, clenching my fists, trying to put his

words back into the Hidden Place of my mind.

I can't carry John with me, and I shouldn't leave him alone again, not after what happened before. The shadows might get to him, might take him from me, and I need to stop them.

"It's all right," John says, slumped against the tree. His eyes shine at me, cotton white, and I can see the ground through his body. "Go get him. I'll be waiting here for you."

I don't have any other choice. If I see the things Mr. Spencer buried, will I ever be able to forget them?

"I'll be back soon."

I wish I still had the flashlight to give him. I wish there was anything else I could do.

I run across the stream, balancing on the tree trunk. On the other side, the earth is soft and wet weeds wrap around my ankles, but I kick them off, chasing after Mr. Spencer as he ducks and weaves through the trees. I'm faster than he is. He hasn't run in years, and he limps along, breathing heavily until he comes to that familiar clearing with a stone marker in the center. The ribbons and metal stars hanging from the branches that were swaying softly when I first arrived here are battling against the wind. I can see the old damaged trees in the woods, cut by the tear of light when Ms. Eldridge was just a girl.

Mr. Spencer stops to catch his breath. The light moves through the woods, getting farther and farther from the Society. Shining through the tree branches, it paints shadows across his face, a glowing triangle on his cheek, fire in his eyes.

The rain pours around us. I look around and see the shadows surrounding us, filling the trees, blowing with the wind.

Mr. Spencer wraps his hands around the stone marker with the star carved in the middle. He wipes the water from his eyes and when he speaks, his voice is gentler than I've ever heard before.

"We don't have to do this anymore. The flu hit your family hard. I'm sorry, Liza. Your parents went first and then John fell ill, but you never got sick."

"No. No, that's not true."

He points through the trees.

"I'll prove it to you. Come with me. I buried the papers over there."

"Stop talking," I say, and pick up a stick, swing it at him, the air *whooshing* around us.

"What are you—"

I swing it again and again until he snatches it from my hand, then I lunge at him and grab the wet fabric of his suit jacket. He spins in the mud and falls, kicking his legs.

"Think hard, Liza. You know what happened."

I try to remember life before the sickness came, those perfect days bathed in sunlight. My memories are like the glimpses of the other side, perfect and warm. But then the stories came from the city, stories of the flu working their way to our small town. I remember when Mother and Father got sick, and then the doctors came and then—

No. No, no, no.

"A part of you must know it," Mr. Spencer says, pulling himself up. "You must."

"Please," I say. "We can leave now. I'll get John and we'll go with you. We'll do whatever you say from now on. I'll never disobey again. I promise."

"You've promised me that before."

Mr. Spencer looks around at the trees. He must see the shadows too. They're everywhere, standing at the edge of the clearing, watching us, waiting.

The storm feels like it's tightening around us, so loud that Mr. Spencer needs to yell so I can hear him. He pulls himself up, and he leans against the stone marker. Half of his body is caked in mud, and his beard hangs in a limp tangle down to his collar.

"I'm sorry I'm the only family you have. I'm sorry it wasn't *me* who got sick. Your parents were the best of us. I'd trade places with them if I could. I can't take care of a child. I didn't want it, either, can hardly take care of myself. Look at me."

It's unlike him to speak so honestly, and it makes me uncomfortable. I prefer when he's just telling his lies.

"Just stop," I beg. "Please don't say any more."

"Then you started talking to *him*, and I thought it was just a game you played, but it never stopped. It was as if you thought John was right there beside you. On and on it went until I realized you actually believed it."

When John got sick, I sat by his bed, praying for a miracle. What was it our parents used to say about us? *One soul in two bodies.*

It can't be true. I think back to when I told Charles that the shadows were after John.

Who? he asked me. At the time, I thought he was asking about the shadows, but could it be that—

No.

"I thought if I kept you silent and hidden from others, I could keep you safe. The world isn't kind to girls who see things. But this place is different. That first day in the chapel, Ms. Eldridge spoke to John, almost like she saw him, too. Or was it Annabelle?" Mr. Spencer gives a sad smile. "It was almost enough to make a believer out of me. I didn't know what they were playing at, Eldridge and her cousin, but I knew

I had to hide anything I had. That Charles fellow was likely to search through my things and start asking questions. What else could I do? But I'm done pretending, Liza. I'm done trying to protect you."

He pulls himself to his feet and turns toward the trees. Before I can protest, the storm blows a powerful gust and knocks us to our feet. The trees bend and there's a loud crack as one begins to teeter, and by the time I realize it's falling, it's too late to escape. It crashes down in the clearing, hitting Mr. Spencer and pinning my legs underneath it. I scream to the sky and it answers with more rain, battering the earth around me. The pain is so great that for a moment I don't think of the storm, can only feel the throbbing throughout my body. I lay my head against the wet ground and close my eyes.

The light is moving through the woods, taking over my vision. I see the shapes move closer and I claw at the ground. The tree is heavy, but the ground is soft enough that I can dig around it with my fingers. I try to wiggle my feet, but the pain is so strong.

I need to get back to him before the shadows get to him. They can't take him, not yet.

I dig harder, scooping up heaps of dirt, trying to free myself. Blood runs down my ankle, and I can barely move my foot without the pain racing through my body.

I look around the tree for Mr. Spencer, but can't

see him. What was it he said to me? I can't remember now. Or maybe I don't want to remember. I put the words back into my Hidden Place, rearrange the world to fit my own truth.

Don't think. Don't think.

There's no time to waste.

My legs come free and I pull myself up, unsteady. The light is so close that I can hardly see the dark world around it. All that remains of my side is a stain at the edges. The light grows as it tears through, a hole punched into the night, and I turn and try to run from it.

That's when I see a woman walking toward me in the night, holding a lantern. Shadows surround her. Through the waves of rain I see her face. It's Ms. Eldridge. Her clothes are soaked through and her gray hair is unclipped, the wet strands blowing down across her shoulders. She steps into the clearing and the shadows that were waiting at the edge follow her.

"It's time, Liza," she says, and takes my hand and motions toward the light.

Another gust of wind comes. It blows out the flame of her lantern and makes the hanging metal stars bang against each other.

"Annabelle!" she announces. "She's here. Show her."

More details begin to take shape in the light. A woman appears, as if lit from behind by the sun.

"I can't be the one to let him go. You have to do it," Ms. Eldridge says. "It's the only way to fix this."

I try to yell but the storm is too loud, and the buzzing sound comes into my ears.

The woman watches us, raising her hands, and the light expands around her, eating up the trees, a hole opening between our world and hers. It slices across the wet, gray ground, getting wider and wider until it covers everything around it.

The light feels like a blanket being pulled around me. I'm caught inside it, stepping into the sun. My cold body feels like it's melting, then evaporating into mist. The pain leaves me. I'm still in these woods, but the trees are bright and golden, and the leaves are green and full. The dark clouds have faded and the smells in the air are sweet. The sky is a brilliant blue and the light shines across every surface.

I spin around, drink it in, feel the warmth on my face. There's a slice of darkness floating behind me, a window back into the other side where the storm still rages. Shadows pour through the opening, and when they pass through, they reverse from shadow to light.

I look around and see the blurred shape of Ms.

Eldridge watching me from the darkness of the other side.

"I'm scared," I say. "Will you come with me?"

"No, dear. You must do this alone."

THE OTHER SIDE

A woman reaches out and takes my hand. Her fingers are warm, and her face is so bright I can hardly look at it.

"It's a delicate thing, this barrier between our worlds," she says. Her voice is smooth, like the one I heard that first morning in the assembly hall. "It must be fixed now."

People surround us, as brilliant and bright as the shadows were dark, and there is beauty all around me.

"Are you Annabelle?"

The woman smiles but doesn't answer.

"What is this place?"

"We have no name for it here. Call it what you wish."

"Am I dead?"

"Haven't you learned by now that we don't use that word? You're only visiting. Look."

She points to my arms and I see that I'm not like the others around us. I'm a shadow now, the reverse of what I was on the other side. I can see through my fingers, straight to the ground, and when my hair falls across my eyes, it's a brilliant white.

"Come."

She leads me through the woods. There are no weeds anymore, and the leaves and the stones on the ground are smooth as glass. We cross the stream. It's calm and bubbling, and minnows circle in the current.

The woods are different, but familiar somehow, and when we walk out of them, I can see down the hill where the Silver Star Society should be. The spot is empty, just a field of long green grass, rising and falling like waves in the gentle breeze, and a little pile of stones where the tear hit the wall, like a marker to the other side.

"The house is gone," I say.

"It was never here. There's no need for buildings."

Horses graze in the field. Birds circle above in a perfect sky filled with clouds that look like balls of cotton.

There are crowds of people around the open field, each glowing in the sunlight.

"They come to this spot to speak through me. My connection to the other side is strong, but *yours*, little one . . . it crashed the worlds together and tore a hole right between them."

"John," I whisper.

"Yes. He was stuck between the two, neither on one side nor the other."

I remember the days back home when the world seemed to dim, and our mother and father slipped away, and all the glow leaves my memories. I think of John in his bed, and how suddenly the coughing stopped. I prayed for him to get better, for a miracle to come.

"Stay with me," I begged him. "I need you."

And he did.

"When you entered this place, you brought the living and spirits too close together," the woman continues. She kneels beside me and I look into her eyes, shining and green. "He broke the barrier. It's fragile, this connection between the worlds, and it must be protected. Some of us have tried to bring him here where he belongs, to separate the worlds, but you wouldn't let us, would you?"

Tears stream down my face. All this time. I knew, didn't I? Deep down, I must have.

"The decision is yours. You must be the one to bring him, to let him stay with us."

"But he needs me," I say. "I love him."

She smiles at me.

"You can love something you can't touch."

We walk further down into the valley. A patch of violet flowers, Mother's favorite, sway in the wind. The beauty is too much to understand. I have so many questions I want to ask Annabelle, but nothing forms on my lips, and it's her that asks me a question first.

"Do you know what you must do?"

I still can't speak, but I do. *I do.*

The figures from the valley begin to walk to me, their feet floating over the glowing grass, coming closer, closer.

"Then it's time for you to go."

No. I want to stay here too. I want to bring John and be here forever, I want to—

She takes my hand and leads me up the valley, into the trees. As we walk, more figures join, stepping out from the limbs and trunks, and the light from their bodies swarms around us, shimmering, filling the woods until we're back at the clearing.

"We'll be waiting."

The dark spot is still there, right where I left it, like the air has been cut with a knife, sliced through. I can see the other side, a world that's gray and loud. I can hear the pouring of rain, the howl of the wind.

Lifting my leg, I step through the tear, back to the darkness, back to the living. As it passes through, the trail of blood reappears around my ankle and the pain returns. I gasp at how quickly it comes, how strong it feels. I lean forward and fall back through the thin place, landing on the wet ground, the storm still raging around me.

Where are you, John?

I'm here. Find me.

A figure hovers above me and I reach out to it, but it's no shadow—it's Ms. Eldridge. She takes my hand and pulls me to my feet. We're beside that massive fallen tree that pinned me down, and the ground is empty underneath it.

"Where's Mr. Spencer?" I ask. The words he said to me echo in my head.

John's dead, Liza. He was gone before you ever came to me.

"I don't know, child. We'll search for him later," Ms. Eldridge says, trying to speak over the storm. She relights her lantern and hands it to me. I begin to walk, through the path and over the trunk that fell over the stream. I try to spot familiar trees and markers, but the storm has broken limbs and washed mud across the path. Nothing looks the same now, even when I arrive at the place where I left John.

Where are you?

I move on, pushing through the branches. I'm soaked to the bone and the rain slides off me. My mind calls to him, over and over, as loud as it can through the growling storm.

John! John!

Shadows appear, surrounding me. They don't frighten me anymore. They blow in the wind, pointing me in the right direction, and I follow them, straining to hear his voice.

Liza . . .

The sound is faint, and I follow it, running now, over broken trees and piles of leaves.

I see him, deeper in the woods, and I run to him, wrap my arms around his fading shape.

"Why didn't you stay at the tree?" I ask, but he doesn't answer. He looks down at the ground beneath him. It's covered in weeds and plants except for one small spot, a foot tall and wide, covered with a mound of fresh dirt.

"This is what Mr. Spencer told you he buried. This is what you need to see."

How does he know what Mr. Spencer said? But of course, he does. He knows because I know.

We're ten feet from the edge of the woods, near a large rock, right where I saw him burying something that first time I went out to meet George.

"Look at it, Liza. Do it for me. Remember it this time."

I fall to my hands and knees and push my hands into the dirt, scooping out handfuls. The earth is soft, and I dig deeper down, pushing it aside until I feel a cold metal box. I claw around the edges and pull it out.

I lay the box on the ground and trace my fingers around the lid, leading to the clasp that holds it shut.

"You already know what's inside," John says. "Don't be scared."

I flip open the lid and my family's faces greet me. It's that photograph John told me about, taken by Mr. Spencer, the summer before the sickness came. I remember his visit now. Mother and Father are sitting on the top step of our house's front porch, with John and me in front of them. He looks so different than the boy beside me now, and the memory of that moment comes back to me in a rush.

Yes. I remember now.

There are more papers underneath it. Letters from my parents to Mr. Spencer, asking him to be there for us should the worst happen, and news articles, doctor's bills, death notices, and papers from the courts stating that I was under his guardianship.

Only my name on the paperwork.

"Did you always know?" I ask John, and he smiles.

"You asked me to stay."

"I know, but I can't ask that of you anymore."

The shadows surround us, and John steps toward them.

We walk together, hand in hand, back to Ms. Eldridge.

She kneels and wipes the tears from my eyes.

"Are you ready?" she asks.

"No."

I'll never be ready.

I lead John back to the light. It pulses with the storm, and it sends out a burst that slices through the ground, showing the brightness of the other side.

"You've been carrying me with you for so long," John says, hugging me tight. "It's time to let me go."

I love you.

I love you, too.

I release his hand and he follows the shadows back into the light, stepping through the thin place, breaking apart into bits of fire, like embers blowing in the wind before re-forming into a perfect shape.

The ball of light fades, closing the tear in the thin place, and I collapse on the ground. The rain hammers on.

A pain shoots through me, filling my body, taking up all the space inside me. I fall to the ground weeping, and water pools around me. When I open my eyes, Ms. Eldridge hunches over me, scooping me into her arms and leading me through the storm, down the valley to the house. I want to scream out, tell her to leave me, but I don't have any fight left.

The house is still standing solid against the wind and rain. Charles and some of the men are boarding over the front, bracing themselves against the wind as they hammer planks to the windows and broken door. When Charles sees me, he runs to us, takes me from Ms. Eldridge and brings me into the house.

Charles carries me up the stairs to a room and lays me on a bed with white sheets, piling soft blankets on top of me. I shiver the cold away. The rain pounds against the little window. It sounds like a lullaby, a gentle song being sung outside. Noise without meaning.

When I sleep, I dream I am on a small boat, only big enough for one person, rocking in the ocean, moving on to somewhere new.

Are you there, John? I call out, alone on the waves, but he doesn't answer.

A Moment Saved Forever

Light streams through my window and wakes me. It's morning. The storm has passed us, and through the little window in my room I see that the sky has turned pink and gold, and birds fly in circles over the Silver Star Society.

Guests walk in the yard, looking at the damage to the building. Branches and leaves cover the stone wall, and the ground is peppered with bricks and shingles, shards of broken glass and wood. The tear in the thin place has left a trail of destruction behind it. Ripped trees show where I entered the woods and led it away from the house.

"You're awake," a voice says, and I turn to see Ms. Eldridge in the doorway, watching me.

"It's all over," she says, coming inside and sitting on the side of the bed. "We've survived the storm, and I believe we'll live to survive another."

Together, we stare at the sky, warmed in the light, and the silence between us is a comfortable thing.

Finally, I ask, "When did you know about John?" and his name catches in my throat.

"When Charles carried you in, I felt there was a presence attached to you. I must say, I never expected it to be so strong."

"I'm sorry," I whisper, but she reaches up and grabs my shoulder, her strong hand pulling me tight.

"It isn't your fault, Liza. There is nothing in this world more powerful than love, and I knew the risks involved."

I nod, and tears stream down my cheeks.

"Everything I've done since you arrived was meant to draw John out and deliver him to where he should be. Of course, to do that, we had to keep Mr. Spencer around and see where it led. Your work was very good. You have nimble fingers and a curious mind, despite the fraudulent nature of your act. I explained it all to Charles and the guests last night. They understood. Most of them, anyway. As for Mr. Spencer . . ."

"Is he still here?" I ask.

She pauses, considers what to say.

"Men have been in the woods all morning looking. We haven't been able to locate him yet, though that might be for the best. Those that have been tricked are perhaps a little *too* eager to find him. For his sake, I hope he's gone for good."

So much has happened since last night that I nearly

forgot about the guests closing around us, chanting *fraud* when the contents of my Hidden Place were dumped on the floor.

"What happened to the detective?" I ask.

Ms. Eldridge smiles.

"He's gone, content in the fact that spirit photography is a lie and that Mr. Spencer's reputation is ruined. Some people will never believe, even things they've seen with their own eyes. It's not our job to convince them."

"I was on the other side," I whisper. "I saw it all."

"Someday you'll tell me all about it," Ms. Eldridge says. "For now, I'd like you to rest. Join us downstairs when you're ready."

I close my eyes, sink into the blankets, let the warmth and light wash over me.

Search parties look for Mr. Spencer all morning and into the early afternoon. When they return, I hear their voices drift up through the house. He wasn't under the fallen tree. They took axes up to that spot in the woods and cleared it away, then rehung the metal stars on branches around Anabelle's stone marker. There was no sign of him in the woods—no ripped fabric from his clothes, no trail of blood or footprints. They told me the rain had washed it all away, but it makes me wonder. Did he ever make it out of the woods? Is he traveling the country with a different name, moving on to stop number twenty? Maybe the truth is simpler. Maybe they're lying to me the same way I lied to them.

John? Can you hear me? I think. If he lived in my mind, I hope a part of him is still there.

I don't want to leave this bed. It's almost as if my new life will start the moment my feet hit the floor, and I don't know how to exist in this strange new world without him.

Please say something, I call out.

"Liza!"

I hear the voice, so clear and real that I sit up in bed.

John!

"Liza! Are you there?"

I run to the window, see a small figure running in the yard, pushing his way through groups of guests, calling my name.

George.

He goes from guest to guest, asking about me, showing the folded picture that I gave him, and a woman points up to the house. He goes to the front porch and climbs over the broken stairs.

Someone has bandaged my leg while I slept and each step is painful, but I ignore it and limp along the hall, clutching the bannister on the way down the staircase and to the front door.

"George!" I yell, and when he sees me, he runs and hugs me.

"That was some storm, wasn't it?"

"It was," I say, holding him close.

"Half our barn got blown away and I was afraid that you were—"

He lets go and examines my leg.

"What happened?"

"I went out in it. I tried to make it to your barn but then . . . well . . . I'm not sure you'd believe it."

I take the picture from his hand and study it, see that it is just me, wrapped in the cotton swirls of the first ghost I ever made.

"That's all right. Tell me anyway. I like your stories."

Fox appears from the side of the house and runs to me. I rub the space between her eyes and her small body quivers with excitement.

"He's not here anymore," I whisper, but that doesn't seem to matter. She follows me as I lead George around the yard, showing him the Society.

We step over pieces of broken glass and chunks of shingles that were ripped off in the storm. Guests stop and stare, watching me like I am some mythical creature, something different and strange, and I suppose I am. I don't have to pretend anymore.

The back door to the basement is open, and Charles is mopping out the water, a deep brown sludge that muddies the grass.

Through the door, I see photographs hanging from a string along the rafters, proof of the lies I once told. Spots of water drip down the papers, and in the sunlight, the ghosts I made look silly and small. I know now how wrong it is to give people memories of their loved ones that never happened. I will tell the truth from now on. To myself, especially.

I promise, John.

George and I sit together on the porch. The sun starts to lower in the sky, sending beautiful red light across the valley. The trees sparkle like they're made of gold, almost like a glimpse of the other side here on earth.

I tell George some of what happened, and I think he believes me.

Charles steps out of the house holding his camera and tripod. He tilts his head, eyeing our position in the light.

"A little over," he says.

I move close to George and smile. Together, we look toward the black lens of the camera, and when the shutter clicks, our image is burned forever onto a glass plate, a moment saved forever.

George stays a bit longer, even though I know his mother and father wouldn't approve of his being here.

"I said I was out looking for firewood. Lots of trees are down and winter will be here soon. I should go home before they come searching."

Home.

There's a tightness in my chest as I remember that I have nowhere to go.

Ms. Eldridge claps her hands behind us, and the guests look to her. Dinner will be ready soon, she says, though it's a simpler meal because the kitchen windows broke and the pantry flooded, ruining much of the supplies.

Guests file into the house, and when Ms. Eldridge passes me, she looks down and says, "You will stay here, Liza. The Society is your home now."

It's not a question, so I don't answer.

"I'll come back and visit!" George says with excitement, then heads up the road and to the woods.

A carriage pulls up from in front of the house and the family that was caught in the storm climbs inside. The boy, William, waves at me and pushes his face against the glass window. He breathes, creating a wisp of fog, then draws a heart with his finger and leans into his sister. In that moment, I'm filled with hope. Hope that things will get better. Hope that I'll make it in this new world.

That night, I work with Charles in the darkroom, developing the final pictures that Mr. Spencer took and the one of me and George.

"We have a lot of supplies left," he says, his eyes twinkling. "What should we use them on?"

In a tray of liquid, I watch as the form of my face takes shape, developing from shadows to light.

"Good memories," I say. "Real ones."

Charles nods, and when the enlargements are made and the papers are ready, he carries them down to the basement and clips them to the string amongst the others. I settle into my room. The floor is still wet, so my suitcase is propped on a chair, opened wide. Everything inside is stacked on a surface or hung to dry. I have no Hidden Place anymore, no more stories to tell, no paper ghosts to make.

I lie in bed and look out the door at the image on the string, the one of me and George on the porch smiling. A little truth amongst the lies.

EPILOGUE

I've been at the Silver Star Society for longer than I'd care to tell you. There never was a stop number twenty for me, and at this point, probably never will be. I don't run away anymore. I don't need to. This is my home now, and I've committed myself to the mission of this place. Guests have come and gone, and I've seen it all in my time—the frauds and the faithful, the fights and the friendships, the sunlight and storms.

The times have changed. Horses don't fill the courtyard much these days. Guests drive automobiles, but their numbers dwindle each year, even as houses are built in the valley, all the way up to the woods, surrounding the stone wall on all sides and filling this place with families and love.

Visitors bring cameras with them, loaded with film, taking pictures of everything in the house like it's a circus attraction, and nothing more. I often wonder how many actually have faith in the other side, that there are spirits out there, waiting for them.

When Ms. Eldridge passed over one cold winter's morning, the Silver Star Society began to feel like everywhere else, and some days I look back and wonder: Did I really see the shadows? Did I step over for a time?

I've lied to myself before.

Some days I feel like Charles, doubting everything. He was as close to a father as I ever had after my own, and a picture of him hangs in the entryway of the house. He's leaning against the stone wall after it was rebuilt, that small smile peeking out from underneath his mustache. Other days, I feel like Margaret, believing it all without question. Maybe I'm a little bit of both.

That old camera of mine sits in the upstairs hallway on a wooden tripod, little more than a decoration now. Above it is the picture of me and George on the porch, framed, and if you squint your eyes and tilt your head, you can almost see a shape beside me, and an arm wrapped around my shoulder, a little cowlick of hair sprouting from the top, but maybe that's just my mind playing tricks.

Still, I know what happened that day, and what I

saw. With each passing year, the space between the living and the spirits feels thinner to me. I see people I once knew everywhere I look. Sometimes, shadows paint the walls at night, little white eyes hovering above me, and I wonder if they're coming for me.

My memories hang in my mind like pictures, clipped on a string that's draped from edge to edge. Not all of them are clear. Sometimes, storms shake them loose, or a blur appears where it shouldn't, but I do my best to remember what's real and what isn't. With a twist of my fingers, I can reach up, pull a picture down, and be in that moment again.

This evening, the air is chilled, and the wind blows down into the valley, whistling through the houses and crisscrossing streets. I creep out past the metal gate, hiking up my dress as I walk through gardens and yards and into the woods. I know the paths, the rocks, the streams. I know the way to the house where George's family still lives, and the spot where we buried my secrets long ago. I work my way through the trees to the little clearing and wipe the moss from the stone marker, check the strings on the silver stars that hang from the branches. They're old and rusted, but still make beautiful sounds when they bump into each other.

It's peaceful here, a Hidden Place of its own. I can

feel the thinness of this place, more and more each day.

Sometimes, when it's quiet, I call out to him.

John? Are you there?

And tonight, when I listen closely, I can finally hear his voice.

ACKNOWLEDGMENTS

In February of 2020, I sat in a restaurant with my agent, Alex Slater, and discussed the idea for a book around a Spiritualist community post-World War I and the 1918 influenza pandemic. While its timing with world events was coincidental, this book helped me focus my energy and provided a sense of stability through unstable times. Thank you, Alex, for being the first to read this book, the first to believe in it, and for the years of support.

Thank you to the entire Little Bee/Yellow Jacket team: Charlie Ilgunas, for always knowing how to improve a story, Natalie Padberg Bartoo, for the design of the book, and Paul Crichton and Tristan Lueck, for their never-ending work getting books into children's hands.

I would like to thank early readers for providing insights and suggestions that helped shape this story: J.W. Ocker, Cliff Lewis, Kelley Rose Waller, Robert Swartwood, and John Cashman. This book would still be in a box and undeveloped (probably broken in shards) without your help.

Special thanks to Matthew Quickel, my creative sounding board, for his encouragement, honesty, and knowing when to push me harder.

While the Silver Star Society is my creation, it was made from a loose combination of Lily Dale in New York and Camp Silver Belle in Ephrata, PA. Thank you to the Lancaster County Historical Society for providing the initial spark for this story, as well as publications from The Historical Society of the Cocalico Valley.

The images in this book were created by using my own photography, stock assets, and public domain images from the Library of Congress's collection, a tremendous historical collection that I urge everyone to explore.

Thank you to my parents, for always believing in me.

And of course, love and thanks to Andrea, Wyatt, Everett, and Marlowe. I couldn't do it without you.